Gran's asleep in the chair. Snoring like she does, though reckons she doesn't.

I don't like leaving her on her own. But I'm bored brainless when I'm with her. And guilty, when I'm not.

She wakes all of a sudden. Gradually comes to. Starts talking.

'I don't know what I'd do without you,' she says, sitting there.

Says she doesn't know where the years have gone. Can't believe I'll be out to work next year.

She's heard there's jobs going at Farr's, the workwear factory. Says p'raps I'll be able to get something down there.

But I don't want to work at Farr's. I'd rather have me eyes eaten out by maggots than work at Farr's.

She doesn't understand that, though.

'You're not in a position to turn your nose up at anythin',' she says. 'And what d'you *think* you're goin' to be? The Prime Minister?'

'Course not,' I say. But I *do* want to be *somebody* . . .

from The Women's Press

Sandra Chick is the author of *Push Me, Pull Me* (Livewire, 1987), winner of *The Other Award* for Progressive Children's Literature, a Feminist Book Fortnight 'Selected Twenty' title and shortlisted for *The Observer* Teenage Fiction Prize 1987; *I Never Told Her I Loved Her* (Livewire, 1989); and *On the Rocks* (Livewire, 1996).

Cheap Street

Sandra Chick

CAVAN COUNTY LIBRARY
ACC. No. C103931
CLASS No. J(TA) 12-14
INVOICE NO. 4583 IES
PRICE £4.99

Cavan County Library
Withdrawn Stock

First published by Livewire Books, The Women's Press Ltd, 1998
A member of the Namara Group
34 Great Sutton Street, London EC1V 0DX

Copyright © Sandra Chick 1998

The right of Sandra Chick to be identified as the author of this work has
been asserted by her in accordance with the Copyright, Designs and
Patents Act 1988.

British Library Cataloguing-in-Publication Data
A catalogue record for this book is available from the British Library.

This book is sold subject to the condition that it shall not, by way of
trade or otherwise, be lent, re-sold, hired out, or otherwise circulated
without the Publisher's prior consent in any form of binding or cover
other than that in which it is published and without a similar condition
including this condition being imposed on the subsequent purchaser.

ISBN 0 7043 4949 3

Typeset in Bembo by F.S.H.
Printed and bound in Great Britain by Cox & Wyman Ltd

Dedicated to Nevil, Georgia and Lola

Part One

One

It's been said, that somewhere between the labour ward and the benefit office, me mother lost her spark; her zest for life. She certainly lost her maternal instincts. And her sense of humour. Miserable cow.

From up here, on the bridge, I can see right across to where she lives. Well, if I lean over into the stinging nettles, hang on tight to the wall, I can. That's why I'm plastered in this dust and other muck – because the wall's crumbling, falling to bits and I've been hanging over it, watching. Wondering. 'Danger!' it says, back there on the path. 'No Entry!' But I don't reckon it's that bad; like, it's not going to collapse *right now* or anything. Be just my luck if it did, mind.

I lean over again. I can't pick her place out clearly, just more or less. Somewhere amidst the greyness, a splodge of turquoise paintwork in the misty rain.

3

She lives on the estate that joins this one.

'If you can call it *living*,' she'd say. A mass of sprawling pre-fabs, semis and terraced maisonettes. A concrete-cancer jungle. Where everyone's had their share of grief. Where everyone's had *enough*. Where people do what they can and what they have to. Surviving, despite the frustration.

Me mother says, that what she can't stand is how nothing ever changes. How you can see people's lives mapped out, 'crib to coffin'. And she's right.

I wonder what she's doing ... But I mustn't. Not for long; I'm determined not to *care*. If you don't *care*, nothing matters; no one can get to you. It's no use being soft. I've known people before who're soft. Soft as shit. And what happens to them? Nothing, that's what. They don't get anywhere – not today, not tomorrow, not ever. Just get trampled on.

Anyway, I live here now, with me gran. Just moved in, a while back. Because me mother's otherwise engaged. With her bloke. *Dan*. Dan the Man.

To start, she said there was nothing in it; that he was 'just a fella'. Said that it didn't mean anything, nothing special. And I believed her. But she was lying.

She said I didn't have to leave, but she didn't beg me to stay. Said a lot of things, but *he* was pulling all the strings.

I cross to the other side of the bridge, look down. A couple of kids are playing on the tip. Little lads, maybe five or six years old. Swinging from a rope, caught over the branch of a puny, leafless tree that might snap at any minute. Snap them, too, if they hit the deck. But they aren't bothered. Giggling turning to laughter, then

4

shouting. All gob. Like me, some people'd say. 'Too lippy for your own good,' – 'Lisa Brunt – always has to have the last word.' But me gran says, 'Quite right, too. Let 'em know you're no pushover.' At least *she's* on my side. Me star player, is me gran.

The two lads meet the dirt with a thud. Swearing, picking themselves up.

'I nearly broke me bloody neck!'

'You *never* – *I* nearly did. *And* me leg.'

'Well *I* nearly cracked me head open ... '

'Oh yeah ... '

They start turning over the rubbish that's been dumped. Sifting through it like professionals, seeing what they can find. Loads of people come down here, scratching around. Sometimes you'll find something good enough to use, or better still, sell. But you've got to be quick or some other git'll beat you to it; have it from your hands before you know it.

It's not a proper tip. Just somewhere where people get rid of stuff – if they haven't got a van and can't get down to the council one. Or if they don't feel like it, can't be bothered. Sometimes you'll get people from outside the estate dumping what they think is junk. That's usually where the good stuff comes from; the sellable stuff. People haul it round the car-boot sales with other bits and pieces they've picked up along the way. Some suckers'll buy anything.

Pickings are poor just now though. A stained mattress, a ripped armchair and an old veneered wardrobe with the sides bashed in. A few cardboard boxes, mushy with the wet, stuffed with old bedclothes and rubbish.

A rusted-out Ford Capri has gradually been taken to

5

bits – it's got no bonnet, no engine and no wheels, just the black vinyl seats, left in a shell. Younger kids play in it by day. Older kids do what they like in it by night. Pete-the-pie-man caught his daughter in there with a lad. Went ballistic, he did – threatened to put him in hospital.

'You and who else, old fella!' the lad said, taking the mick, and Pete got his hands round his throat.

'I'll beat your bloody lights out! I *will*, mind ... I *will* ...' His wife had to drag him off and everybody thought it was a bit of a laugh. 'I'll *'ave 'im* ...' he's ranting.

'Don't hurt 'im, Pete!' his wife's going. 'It's not worth it – don't hurt 'im!'

'Hurt 'im? *Hurt* 'im? I'll dance on the bugger's grave singing halle-bloody-lujah if I have to!'

It's a standing joke now, what goes on inside the Capri after dark; the *passion wagon*.

The smaller of the two boys shouts out. 'Bollocks! I've cut meself!' Wipes blood from his hand onto his pale and grubby football shirt.

'What d'you do that for, divvy?' his pal laughs, matter of fact.

'Shut it,' he says, close to tears. Looking up at me, watching. 'And what're *you* gawping at? Get lost.'

'Don't boss your elders,' I say and smile. Poor kid – looks a right loser, standing there bleeding on other people's dirt, other people's grime.

But the estates are just one big dumping ground. A dumping ground for humans; though some people don't think we are human. Talk about us as if we're crawling the walls, infesting their air. 'It's not the place, it's them that live there ... ' That's what the snobs up Laurel Park say; the nearest *private* estate. Full of self importance and crap.

Gran says they're vile 'I'm all right Jack' people, that talk out of their backsides. I can see *them* from the bridge, as well. Just about. All creamy and clean in the distance. Fenced and fancy. Two ups, two downs; too frilly and fussy. Neat little borders – dug and planted by snotty little men with pressed trousers, crisp shirts and jobs.

I can see a lot from up here. That's why I like it. And nobody hassles you. Might see a few kids, messing around, or somebody walking their dogs. No trains any more, though. Haven't been any trains for years – or, I can't remember any. All wild and wasted now.

Still. I've got t' get going, or Her Royal Highness'll have a fit.

The quickest way back to Gran's place, is to cut through Avondale Road. Past the chippy, the betting shop, the open-all-hours shop.

They've got a sign up outside today – 'Special Offer! Free ride in a police car for all shoplifters! Age/status no object!' Everyone goes in there looking to nick stuff – it's dead easy.

It's where a lot of kids hang out. Where sad and bitter old dears peer out from behind ragged curtains scolding and cursing 'the youth of today' Where 'the youth of today' give them mouthfuls of abuse – laughing, enjoying the entertainment. Winding them up, spinning them a line for the sake of it.

I heard this old biddy in the shop the other day, 'What they need,' she said, 'is a good war; to get rid of their aggression. That, or the birch.' I mean, what is it with old people? In fact, with anyone over about *thirty*? It's like, every time they open their mouths, complete and utter rubbish comes out. You gotta laugh, though, I s'pose.

It's busy with kids on their way to school. Some dressed in shabby uniform, some just shabby.

A pair of girls are giving rides in a discarded shopping trolley. Whizzing past the gateless gardens and front yards. Pushing, running, then letting go until it crashes.

A little 'un starts bawling, hurt. I don't know them — don't know many people over this way. But know to mind me own business, keep me hooter out.

'Bay-bee,' they taunt her. 'Want your mummy, do ya?' Leaving her on the kerb to sulk, wiping her runny nose in the sleeve of her cardi.

'I'll get me brother for you lot!' she cries.

'Oh, no!' They grin. 'Are we *scared*!'

Turning the corner into Brenner's Close you get a few satellite dishes in your face, dogs and dogshit under your feet. More brats, milling about. Bored, looking for something better to do. Kicking a beer can up the street, making a hell of a din. Tackling each other, falling and knocking into a dustbin. Then kicking the rubbish into the middle of the road.

A bloke is scrubbing his front door. Scrubbing at the words 'Gay Boys', daubed in pink paint. A bucket of soapy water at his feet and a brush in his hand. Scrubbing hard, looking vicious as hell.

Gran's house is further along, in Rodden's Place. She calls it 'bloody *Rodents* Place. Nothing but a rat run,' — because of the bikes and cars, tearing up and down, up and down. Racing and challenging each other. Friday night, Saturday night, any night really. She gets cross with them. 'They'll *kill* somebody one day,' she says. But Gran gets cross with most people for one reason or another.

The two flats opposite are boarded up. Were left empty

and then some kids got in there. 'Druggies', they reckon. Mucking about and wrecking the joint. So now the maintenance department have to get it liveable again, sort it out ... sometime. Sometime, never, probably. Gran gets real worked up about it, says it's a wasted chance for somebody – a couple of young families or something; she wishes they'd get on with it. Though *I* say, who'd want to live there, anyway? Plenty people, she reckons, plenty people. But it just looks like a prison to me. One that's been forgotten. That's what happens here, everything gets forgotten – until there's trouble.

Sometimes we make the local paper. '*The troubled Lyme Grove area ...* ' And so we get the reputation of being a bunch of maniacs, on the rampage. Too low in brain power and too high in sperm count, doing nothing except breeding and sponging off the State. Costing 'decent people' too much money and putting nothing back in return. When a chance would be a fine thing.

I can see Gran. Standing at the window in a duster-yellow tabard and a temper. Plaiting and unplaiting her fingers. Looking dead mean-mouthed as she catches sight of me.

'Lisa! Where the bloody hell have you been?'

Two

Gran has got her arse in her hand because I'm late and she was worried and imagined me dead in a ditch somewhere.

'How was I to know?' she says. 'Anythin' could've happened to you.'

'Could've done. But it didn't, did it?' I say, and she throws me a look. 'Though if it ever does, remember I want *Jerusalem* at me funeral; a good rousing chorus and lots of tears ... enough to wake me up, just in case I'm not *quite* gone.'

'Don't get clever with me,' she says, sharp. Folding her clean laundry, piling it into the manky plastic washing basket. 'And don't be so bleedin' morbid; checky little devil. I thought I'd finished worrying about kids.'

'And then you got landed with me ...'

She shifts about a bit.

'Well. Just you behave yourself; I'll have your guts for garters if you're not careful.'

There's nothing fluffy about Gran. Nothing gransy or mumsy. She makes judgements and statements. Often says about herself, 'Olive Nelson has ample capacity to cope.' Like, full stop. You don't mess with Gran, unless you want a thick ear.

She's fiddling with the knitted chairback on the settee as I flop down into the seat. Straightening the arm covers, pulling them over the worn patches where time has rubbed away the brown woolly finish.

'Get out from under my feet,' she says, picking up her damp, crumpled tea cloth and throwing it at the squawking bird's cage in the corner. 'And that stinking parrot of yours can learn t' shut up, too.'

'It's not a parrot Gran, it's a cockatiel.'

'Parrot or damn cocka–whatsit,' she says. 'All stink the same. Just a budgie with attitude ... ' She drags on her cigarette. 'Don't know why you got the thing ... '

'I told you – someone gave it me.'

'Well, give it back, then,' she says. 'Or let it fly away, never t' be seen again ... '

At least you know where you are with me gran. She doesn't fudge. That's what I admire about her. No bullshit.

She puts her fag down in the ashtray. Sighs, stands for a second, hands on hips; the material of her apron stretched tight across her round, sticky-out stomach. Looks like she might say something deep and utterly meaningless, as usual. But she doesn't say anything.

'I'll boil the kettle, then,' I say.

'You *won't*,' she says.

'Why not?'

'You haven't got time, that's why not.'

'I have … '

'You *haven't*. Get yourself ready for school. And don't take all day.'

She's looking tired. Run down, but hardened to it. Though she gives me the wink – the one that says all is forgiven.

'Do I *have* to go, Gran?'

'Yes,' she says. 'You do. I don't want no official people round here looking for you; *nosing*.'

'They *won't*. They don't worry.'

'You heard what I said. Now come on … '

'But I'll be late now and … '

'*You heard what I said.*'

I wander upstairs. Get me tracky bottoms off and pull on the bobbly green skirt, shaped like a bag-and-a-half of spuds. The milky white shirt that you could spit through; no effort required.

Gran didn't ask me to cover for her this morning; I said I'd do it. She looked worn out; said she felt 'full of years'. And she seemed it, too. Much more than her seventy.

'I could've sworn it was Sunday,' she said, still in her dressing gown, instead of ready and waiting for work.

'It's *Monday*, Gran. Don't you remember, we went down the market yesterday, *Sunday*?'

'Course I remember,' she snapped. 'What d'you think I am? Stupid?'

Said she knows it's only a poxy cleaning job, but she can't afford to lose it; and lose it she would, if she let them down again. I told her that I can run quicker than her – get there, get it done, be back for half past eight, no problem.

There's only a few offices to do, it didn't take me long. And they don't care who does it, as long as everything's spick and span. I didn't even see anyone, so there'll be no complaints.

I hung around a bit after. Just felt like it. Couldn't see the point of rushing back; thought I'd be bound to wangle the day off, somehow. *Dammit.* I'm late now and'll end up with an earful.

I pull on a pair of dirty socks, the heels grey from last week. The baggy green cardi. It'll have to do.

Back downstairs, the clock on the mantelpiece has packed up, sitting there, motionless between a couple of goldy framed photos of family. I push the kitchen door open to check the time. Gran's sat at the table.

'All right?' I say.

'Mind you get some food in you,' she says. 'Have this,' holding out a pound.

'S'all right. I'm not hungry.'

'Take it,' she says. 'You will be, later on.'

I don't argue. 'See you later, then.'

'Watch yourself,' she says, as the door springs shut.

I sling me bag over one shoulder. Smashing it into the cactus plant on the sideboard, knocking it into the bowl of darkening, sweet bananas and soft pears.

'*What the hell's that?*' she calls out.

'I'll clear it up later,' I call back, as she slams the serving hatch open, peering into the front room. 'I *will*, Gran. *Honest.*' And I'm gone.

I hate school. I hate the smell of school. The smell of school dinners. The smell of disappointment and the smell of failure.

The lesson's already started by the time I get there.

13

Tyson's out the front, scrawling on the board. Turns round when he hears me come in.

'I might have guessed,' he sighs, used to it already.

'It's not my fault,' I say, as he peers down at me.

'"It's not my fault, *Sir*,"' he says.

'It's not my fault, *Sir*.'

'Do tell,' he says, dead sarky. 'I'm sure we'd all love to hear more ... '

'Me auntie died last night, Sir,' biting me bottom lip, trying not to give meself away. He hesitates.

'Your auntie? What auntie was that, then?'

'Me auntie ... ' I pick a name. 'Anne.' He hesitates some more.

'Oh dear. And on what side of the family was your Auntie Anne?'

'Me dad's sis ... no, me mum's sister.' Someone at the back starts sniggering.

'Shhh ...,' Tyson says. But he's sussed that I'm blagging him. 'What did she die of?'

'Ummm ... Well, I don't really know.'

'You don't know?'

'I don't know.'

'Lisa Brunt ...' He sighs.

'Honest, Sir,' I say, as the sniggering grows. 'She just died – in the night.' I have to suck me cheeks in to keep a straight face.

'Yes? And so did a fly on my window ledge. Now hurry up and sit down.'

The class are in fits, now.

'It's true, Sir,' I say. 'She did.'

'Sit!' he shouts.

I pull a chair out, the metal legs screeching as they drag

across the tiled floor.

'*Lift it*,' he says. '*Lift it*.'

I plonk meself down, nudging me bag under the desk with one foot. Nick a pencil from Pig, who's sat next to me.

'*Parasite*,' she hisses, as I grab it from the ink well. She's called Pig because she's a pig; her real name's Anita. On the other side I've got the lovely Laura, who makes me want to throw up; full of politeness, promise and potential. A bank clerk, if ever I saw one. She glares at me like I'm some sort of pond life. I give her a sickly smile and follow it quickly with a don't-give-me-any-crap-or-else frown.

And for some reason, I almost start whistling, but manage to stop just in time, before the first note escapes me lips. Which is just as well, because you're not meant to be happy and enjoy yourself here; they wouldn't stand for it.

'Right,' Tyson says, turning to face the class. Which is my cue to switch off.

Start reading the desk. 'Man. City are Bums', 'Newcastle Utd FC', 'Chris 'n' Zoey – 2 gether 4 ever', 'Julie N. is a Tart'. I cross out the 'Julie' and write 'Susan'. That's me mother Susan N.

And she's a tart. Not a proper up-front-on-the-street-tart. She's not that honest about it.

We were all right, y'know. Me and her. When it was just the two of us and everybody left us alone to get on with things. She said we didn't need a *man*; that was one thing she'd learned from having me dad around. But then *he* came along; *Dan the Man*.

She played it down to start with. Played it cool. Then

suddenly, it all changed. Suddenly, he was the best thing that'd ever happened to her. And she wasn't about to pass up the chance of 'a better life' – she said as much. Not for me, not for anyone. The chance of living happily ever after. Well, excuse me while I vomit, *Mother.*

I wanted to talk but she wouldn't listen. All she could do was harp on all the time about how she'd 'never had a hope', being a mum at seventeen, and more or less on her own. How she'd 'never *done* anything ... couldn't *do* anything.' About how powerless she felt. As if everyone else's life's been a crop of red rosebuds all the way.

But when *I* looked at him, all I could see was a creep. A bully. Pushing her around, telling her what to do. When and how to do it. A control freak.

He made me out to be a troublemaker. A stirrer and a problem. Liked to make me look a fool, a dunce. I couldn't do anything right. And she wasn't interested in me any more; I was just in the way, messing things up. After all – Dan works and Dan pays and Dan can offer her something better. So she thinks.

He's her priority now. She's depending on dependable Dan. Doing what *he* wants, to get what *she* wants. And in my book, that makes her a tart.

But what I'd like to know is, if she's so damn happy, why is it that she never smiles?

'*Lisa Brunt!*' Tyson bawls. 'I asked you a question! Wakey, wakey!' I look up. 'Well. Thank you for sparing me some of your time!' he says, against a background of giggling. 'Now. If you don't mind, I'd like you to tell me the estimated populations of the following – Asia, Africa, Australia ... ' And I'd like him to stick his atlas up his arse, but we don't always get what we want, do we?

16

After Tyson, it's the delectable Miss Merryweather for games. Bit of a glamour-puss, they say she's too good for round here. Too 'nice'. But she's nothing special – just because she's got long legs and can wrap her gob around a few vowels.

'Well, where *is* your kit?' she purrs.

'Haven't got any, Miss ... '

She looks at me like she's in pain.

'But *why* haven't you got any?'

'I just haven't.' I carry on, searching through the lost-property bin. Trying to look sad and dejected so she'll feel guilty and let me off.

Does she hell. She sighs, exasperated. 'Hurry up, love.' And I have to wear what's there.

I'm hopeless at games. I *hate* games. And in particular, poncey netball.

'Come on ... Put some effort into it. Can't you catch?' Yes, thank you, I *can* catch. But I don't *want* to. I won't catch just because someone tells me to.

'Look at her *shorts*!' some godly little blonde sneers. 'They're *boy's* ones, aren't they?'

Miss Merryweather sighs some more. She does a lot of sighing.

'What's going to become of you, Lisa? You're never going to get into the team at this rate ... '

Oh, deary me, how sad – top meself, shall I? Slit me throat with a butcher's knife?

Three

As you walk into the block where Mum lives, the sanitised hum of disinfectant smacks you straight in the face. But you know it's filthy. Pissy and cold and filthy.

This is where I grew up. Where I played and ran riot; laughed and screamed. Where sometimes I was happy, and where other times I got me bum kicked. Maybe deserving it, maybe not. Where I used to come a cropper on the concrete steps for a pastime, every day it seemed.

'There you are! I *told* you what'd happen ... You *never* learn!'

That's the trouble with mothers – they know it all. Or think they do.

Our place'll be somebody else's soon. Dan the Man's got his *own* place. A *house*. On the other side of town. Somewhere *better*, away from the stench.

I walk up the stairway; bang on the door.

Nothing.

Then voices. Giggling. A silly scream; a docile reaction. More giggling.

The letter box rattles; opens.

'If it's the catalogue money you're after, I'll pay double next week,' she says.

'It's *me*, Mum,' I say.

'Oh. That's all right, then,' and she turns the key to let me in.

She looks flustered and hot.

'Didn't expect you,' she says – which is obvious – fastening the buttons of her crumpled blouse.

'Who is it?' Dan calls out from the bathroom.

'Only Lise,' she says, and the gushing water of the shower begins to run. She bends down to pick up an envelope that's lying unopened on the mat. 'What's this?' she mumbles to herself.

I walk on through to the kitchen and she follows.

'What've you been up to, then?' she asks, throwing the letter on the side.

'Nothing.'

'How's your gran?' Sticking her hand up under her skirt and pulling her top down.

'She's all right.'

'That's all right, then,' she says. Looks dead un-interested. 'Coffee?'

I shrug. Thinking about what they've been up to. Anything he wanted, I 'spect. I hate to think of them, together, like *that*.

'Yes or no?' she says. I shrug again.

'If you like.'

'Well, don't force yourself … ' She turns round to get

19

the cups, the milk out. Stretches up on tiptoe for the sugar, her shoes slopping off at the heel.

'You can see your pants through that skirt,' I say.

'You *cannot*,' she says, turning back.

'Can. At the back — there's a line, a ridge, right the way around.'

She's put out.

'It's only an old one, anyway ... A cheap one.' Pushing her hands into the lemon cotton pockets, making it worse, tighter. Then,

'Did you hear about Pat?' she says.

'No. What's she done now?'

'Only come up on the lottery,' she says.

'How much? Not big time?'

'She won't let on. But her Kev reckons it's about three thousand quid.'

'Three thousand!'

'Mind you, she's acting like it's three *million*. Had a spend-up in town with her Margaret last Monday. Was splashing it about down the club, Tuesday — and Wednesday, she booked a fortnight in Spain for her and the kids; flying out Saturday week.'

I can't imagine what three thousand quid even looks like.

'Three grand ... ' I say.

'I dunno,' she muses. 'It's like Dan says, you can't really *do* much with that amount. It's not enough, really,' walking to the mirror, picking up a lipstick.

'I'd have a go,' I say.

She rubs the greasy pink colour around her mouth. Puckers her painted lips into a kiss. Runs her fingers over her cheeks, and through her crinkly perm.

She's got a fading yellowy-purple lovebite on her

neck. A sapphire blue rock, surrounded by little glittery chips, on her finger. The third finger of her left hand – and she's holding it out, straight, just the way you don't. But I don't say anything.

She sprays and pats her mousey hair. Then examines her nails, long with chipped varnish. But I refuse to notice her crown jewel.

She makes the coffee, rabbiting on about Mad Sally, next door. About how she goes down to the washing lines dressed in just her bra and pants, for all to see. How she's 'stoned out of her head' on tranquillisers. How she hollers and bawls at her kids.

Mum thinks it's funny; hilarious, in fact. Is laughing as she plonks the mug down on the table, wasting it.

'Bugger,' she says, and wipes it with a damp cloth.

I don't know what to talk about, so I don't say anything and there's this weird silence.

'So,' she says, eventually. 'Your gran must be in her element, now, then ... with you there? Always had a soft spot for *you*. And I bet she spoils you rotten?'

I shrug. 'It's all right.'

'Well,' she says. 'I'm just glad it's all sorted now.' Pulls a face and the lines around her eyes and mouth harden.

'It was *his* fault,' I say.

'Come on,' she says. 'We've been over this a hundred times. It just didn't work ... So let it be, eh?' Then, 'Shhh,' as the bathroom door goes. 'Now don't *start*.'

Dan is washed and dressed: his clean damp hair combed back. But he pulls on the same old dusty overalls, and muddy steel toe-capped boots.

'All right, love?' she fawns; taking on a different air. That of *Dan's woman*.

'All right,' he says. 'Any tea going?'

'Yeah … Hang on.'

He looks at me.

'What you doin' here, then?'

'Nothing.'

'Got any fags, Sue?' he asks.

'In the other room, on the telly,' she answers, and he goes off in search of one.

'Am I not supposed to come and see you any more, then?' I say. But I get the sharp end of the bride's tongue.

'He didn't *mean* anythin'. You always make something out of nothin', you.'

I finish me coffee and go.

Outside, a gang of kids are playing 'Chicken' on the main road. Jumping out in front of the traffic, then back onto the kerb at the last possible moment. Too soon, and the chant goes up, 'chicken, chicken, chicken', or sometimes, 'rent boy, rent boy'.

A couple of girls are hanging around by Hamm's Grocery Store; I know one of them – the wannabe-luscious-Joanne-Kelly – from school. Had trouble with her from day one. They check me out.

'Look at the state of that!' Squawking. 'Look at 'er shoes!'

I don't show any feelings. Not ever. Make out I'm hard – tell them to eff-off – 'cause what else can I do? You got t' stick up for yourself. But they say, both together, 'Why should we?' So I tell them to eff-off again, louder this time, and next thing, I'm sandwiched between the wall and this girl's gob. I push and she pushes and me heart goes berserk as her mate grabs hold of me hair – then this bloke comes storming out of the shop.

'Pack it in, you lot and get lost!' he shouts. And they skip away, laughing as I stand there wondering what's hit me. 'Get out of it!' he says to me. 'Little slags.'

I run all the way home. Stop just in time to get me breath back.

Gran's at the kitchen window. Waiting. I'm all quivery.

'What's the matter with you?'

'Nothing.'

'Barging in. In a hurry or somethin'?'

'No.'

'What've you been doin' then?'

'Nothing.'

I pour a glass of orange. Get the biscuit tin out and dip in.

'Don't fill yourself up on rubbish,' she says. 'It's fruit and veg you need – a young girl like you. And cheese – that's what you want.' She takes her glasses off and rubs her eyes; dark and heavy. Gets up from her chair and takes a cigarette from the packet on the shelf. Switches the front ring of the cooker on, bending over to light up. As she sucks to make it catch, sparky bits float off the end of the fag and she jumps back. 'Nearly had me bloody eyebrows.'

'Gran,' I say. 'You've already got one on the go – over there – in the ashtray.'

'I haven't, have I?'

'I'll have it,' I say.

'Put it *out*,' she says. '*I'll* have it – later.'

She's always doing it – leaving cigarettes about, forgetting about them. I find them, burnt away, a line of whitish-grey ash, on the worktop, on the table, upstairs on the loo. She sits down again. Inhaling deeply, then blowing the smoke out into the cabbagey air. Cabbagey because she's cooking – some stewy, livery concoction with greens. Like, I *can't wait.*

'Seen your mother?'

'Yeah.'

'And?'

'And what? She's all right.'

'Huh,' she says. 'That's a matter of opinion.' Then, 'The trouble with your mother is,' she says, 'she's got ideas above her station. I mean, I just don't know what she's looking for, what she thinks she's going to find.'

'Something better,' I say.

'Like ...?' she says. 'You can't change what you are. *Who* you are.' I just shrug. 'I dunno,' Gran says. 'No. You're best off here, with me.'

I feel like saying, like it or lump it, but know that wouldn't be fair.

I take a drag from her fag, propped up on her saucer.

'Oi,' she says, snatching it back and sticking it between her lips.

'Don't want it anyway,' I say. 'The end's all wet. You always do that, Gran ... '

'Don't be so rude,' she says, winking. Calls out as I walk away, 'And feed that damn parrot before I knock it on the 'ead, will you? Stop its bleedin' screechin' ... '

They say me gran thinks a lot of me. Parrot or no parrot, I s'pose. But it doesn't change anything. I mean, she wouldn't say it in so many words, but I know the truth. That I wasn't one of those kids that was *wanted*; I just happened. Happened and was put up with.

Perhaps there's something about me; something that stops Mum from feeling how mothers are meant to feel about their kids. But it's funny – how I still want to

24

defend her sometimes. Like, it's all right for *me* to criticise her – but if anyone else does it ... It hurts.

I go out to the passage to get the birdseed from the drawer. But with that Natalie, from number twenty-nine, bursts in through the back door. In a right state and a mess – crying and ranting on, nineteen to the dozen.

'He did it again. It's always the same when he's got the drink in him ... ' Her face, around the eye, is red and marked. The corner of her mouth, cut open.

'What's going on?' Gran says, startled. 'What's happened, now?'

'*Him*,' Nat shouts. 'What d'you think?'

'Calm down, Nat,' Gran says. 'Come on ... Calm yourself down.'

'Look at the state of me,' she sobs, bunged up with tears and anger. Clutching the door frame to steady herself.

We stand for a minute, Nat trying to get herself together; Gran rubbing her, gently, on the back.

'Come on ... Come on,' softly.

'Sorry,' Nat says, eventually. 'Sorry.'

'Nothing to be sorry for ... Come on.'

We go through to the front room. Sit down, Gran and Nat huddled together.

'What was it this time, love?' Gran asks her.

'No reason,' she says, still crying, catching her breath. 'Doesn't need a reason, does he? Just got the drink in him – slapped me around a bit ... '

Gran pulls a small flowery hanky from her rolled-up sleeve.

'Here. Wipe your lip.' As it touches her torn skin, Nat winces. 'You're all right, now,' Gran says.

'I must be mad ... ' Nat says. 'Why do I stay with him?''
Running her hands through her short red hair. Holding
herself.

'I dunno, love,' Gran says, quietly. 'I dunno.'

Exhausted, Nat whispers, 'Because there's nowhere else
to go, that's why. I've got no money and there's nowhere
else to go.'

She looks too young, too sad and too used.

Four

They say me dad was a 'skirt-chaser'.

'Just a lad, really,' Gran says. 'And all that lads want is a few pints of beer in their belly and a bit of "oh-be-joyful" from some girl.' Gran can't say *sex*. It's not part of her language. Neither is period (your visitor), penis (his doodah), or vagina (your whatsit).

Gran says, me dad won't have 'made anything of himself'. Says he will have spent his days ducking and diving, his nights breaking hearts and causing havoc.

I don't know where he is. I don't know *who* he is. I know his name's Gary and he came to see me once when I was five, and again when I was six. I remember his brown leather jacket, but I don't remember his face.

Though lately, I wonder about him all the time. Wonder if he's proved them all wrong. Grown up into some glittery millionaire, soaked in cash and kindness.

27

'Oh yeah,' Gran says. 'Giving great wads to charity and leading the life of a saint. Like hell ... '

I wonder if he wonders about me?

'He was just a waster,' she says, 'waiting to happen. Needed his ears boxed. Needed to meet his match.' Gran has standards. He didn't meet them. 'Any man that leaves a young girl with an eight-month-old baby, isn't worth remembering,' she says.

Still. I'd like to see for meself. I'd like to make sure he's as bad as they reckon.

There aren't even any photos. Nothing.

Gran's getting spruced up to go to bingo.

'Believe me,' she says. 'I'm your gran and I know a rotten egg when I see one, agreed?'

I drop the subject, before she gets snotty.

Fighting for mirror space.

'D'you mind, *madam*,' elbowing me out of the way. Her face already thick with orangey-beige foundation cream and cloying powder, she reddens her cheeks with a dab of rouge.

'Rub it in a bit, Gran.'

'Why? Is it too much, then? It's the one I always wear ... '

'It'll be all right – but rub it in more.'

'I don't want it to look too much, but I've got t' use something, be like going out in the nude, otherwise.'

Just imagine – Gran in the nude. Frightening, it is.

I'm digging Pure Plum lip gloss out of a little pot, spreading it on with a finger. Got it from Natalie the other day – she said it'd 'brighten me up'.

'Change me life, will it?' I said.

'Doubt it,' she said. 'But you never know. Won't do you

any harm; make the most of what you've got.'

'What's that new-fangled litter?' Gran says. '*Jam*?'

She's in a good mood – confident of winning the jackpot tonight.

'The others may as well stop at home; I can feel it in me urine.'

She's going with Mary and Jim from next door. Starts panicking when they turn up a nano-second early.

It's all, 'Where's me purse?' 'Where's me specs?' 'Where's me bag?' She can't ever seem to remember where she's left things – then finds them, only to say a few minutes later, 'Where's me purse?'

She's always been a bit like it. Or as far as *I* can remember; had a rubbish memory, repeating herself a lot. And we always thought it was dead funny, taking the mick. Laughing behind our hands; behind her back.

But it's different now.

Before I came to live with her, I used to see her quite often, but never for very long. Stick me head round the door, say hello. Ask if she was okay. She'd say she was fine, have a bit of a chat. She'd always give me a quid – then off I'd go. But living with her is different. And she's starting to drive me nuts. Losing things. Asking the same questions twice or three times. Losing track of the conversation and drifting off. But if I say anything about it, she gets narky. And I haven't said anything to anyone else, 'cause I don't want to upset her, make out she's daft.

Mary smiles.

'All right, then, Lise?' she asks.

'All right,' I say.

'What you up to?'

'Nothin'.'

'Oh ... ' She smiles again.

Her bare legs have the mottled look of corned beef. Her coat is too small, doesn't meet at the buttons; she's holding it together. But her face is pretty – or, you can tell it used to be, once.

Jim stays quiet, behind her. A big bulky man with nothing to do. Hands in pockets, his stomach pokes out of his leatherette jacket, hanging over his trousers. He wears work boots, but has no work.

'Thought you might have found yourself a young man ... ' Mary says, not thinking it for an instant.

'Or a young woman,' Jim says, jokingly. ''Cause you never know these days, do you?'

'*Jim,*' she says. 'Cut it out! That's not funny.' And he blends back into the zig-zaggy wallpaper, or tries to. Mary gives him one of her looks; put out and embarrassed.

'That's the trouble with you,' she says. 'Anything for a cheap laugh.'

Gran appears, rummaging through her shopper.

'Right,' she says. 'Purse, fags, hanky, key. All set for a full house. Where we going – up the Rank?'

'*Rank*?' Mary says. 'That was *years* ago. You mean *The Palace.*'

'That's it,' Gran says. 'That's what I mean – The Palace.'

Mary confides that she's wearing her lucky knickers, and off they go, chattering and hopeful.

I've got nothing to do.

Except sit and watch a gang of girls and lads that're hanging about outside. Wishing *I* had someone to go around with, but I don't. And what with changing schools and all ... But then, there wasn't really anyone at the old place, either. Like there were hundreds of people, but you can still be on your own. And I was. An outsider. It was just me and Mum – versus the rest of them. Versus the world.

I don't want these kids to see me, so I turn the light off.

They're opposite. Trying to get the boards off the windows, get inside. Laughing. Swearing. Taking flying kicks and cursing. Swigging from a labelless bottle, passing it round. Shouting at anyone who walks by, 'Oi ... You ... Wanker ... ' A couple are snogging, groping each other up against the wall ...

Then I wonder if it looks like our place is empty for the evening? If they might try and get in here? I pull the curtain across and switch the light back on, quick.

Just catch sight of a bloke going into Nat's.

Y'know, some people say Nat's on the game. I've heard them, talking about her. They say she *must* be. But most people shut up and say nothing. She's all right, Nat.

Reckons she didn't used to be crazy, but life has a habit of letting her down.

I put the telly on. *Eastenders*. Then there's a bang on the glass and I nearly jump out of me skin. Dive back to the window and look out.

Joey's mud splattered Cabriolet is standing outside.

'Come on,' he calls. 'Let us in.'

I open the door.

He looks rough.

I'm unenthused. The last person I want to see.

'Where's me mother?' he says.

'Out.'

'Where?'

'Bingo.'

'Her and her bloody bingo,' he says. 'What time's she coming back?'

''Bout eleven.'

'*Eleven*? I can't hang about here all night ... '

'No?' I say. 'So there really is a God ...?'

'What?' he says, not getting it.

He pulls a roll of notes from his top inside pocket. Throws a couple of tenners on the sideboard.

'Put it in the pot. And don't get no ideas – make sure she gets it.'

'She *will*.'

'She'd better ... And by the way – don't you go giving her no grief while you're stopping here. Behave yourself, d'you hear?'

'Yes, *Sir*,' I say, flat as a pancake.

He starts nosing through some stuff, chucked on the chair. Electric bill, a letter from the council ... Turns round again.

'Dolled up tonight, aren't we?' Sniggering.

'So?' I say.

'Just tell her I was here,' he says, and I salute. 'And don't forget what I said,' looking at me; smirking and shaking his head.

As soon as he's gone, I'm at the mirror.

I know I look stupid. Feel stupid. Not just plain, but ugly. Rub the back of me hand across the Pure Plum lips – smudging it over me chin. Wipe it off on me cuff. Hate meself.

When Gran comes home she says she was 'close to a big win'.

'Nearly had it, I did. *Just* missed.' Meaning that the

number next to the one she wanted came up.

'You mean, you lost,' I say.

'Don't be cocky,' she says. 'Anyway – there's always next week.'

I tell her that Joey's been. Her voice and her face soften at the mention of his name.

'Oh – I didn't miss him again? Dammit.'

Gran says Joey's a good boy. 'Loyal and constant and fair,' she says. 'A real good boy.'

I give her ten quid and keep ten quid.

Five

First thing, and Gran, Nat and Mary have parked themselves in the street – chinwagging; clutching hold of freshly delivered milk.

Gran is dressed and in her apron, but the other two are in their dressing gowns, Mary with her hair pinned up in pink plastic rollers.

Penny, Mary's daughter, is lurking behind her mother. They're all laughing, joking. All except Penny, who's looking as hacked off as hell.

Mary's complaining that Jim takes her for granted.

'What you've got to understand,' Nat says, in her low gravelly voice, 'is that men aren't like us; they're shallow. And what you've gotta do is – give 'em loads of attention one minute, then *nothin*' the next; ignore 'em completely. That fascinates 'em, that does. They don't understand it – so it gives you that bit of *mystique*.'

Mary looks completely baffled.

'*What*?' And her and Gran laugh their heads off.

'Honest,' Nat says. 'That's the way to keep 'em interested in you. Keep 'em on their toes. You mark my words.' Then, 'I should've been an agony aunt, me,' she says.

'God help us,' Gran says.

'Well, p'raps not, eh? What I *really* fancy being is one of them Marlboro-smoking suicide blonde types ...'

'Like Monroe?' Mary says.

'Oh, no,' Nat says. 'Not like her – 'cause she's *dead*, in't she ... I didn't mean it *literally*.'

They chuckle as Penny butts in.

'Can I have a fiver then, Mum, or not?'

'Oh, change your tune, Pen,' she says. 'How many times do I have to tell you? *I haven't got it t' give you.*'

'You *always* say that.'

'I *know* I do,' gritting her teeth. 'Because that's how it is.'

Penny skulks off. Lifeless and listless. Mary slowly shakes her head.

'Dull as ditch water, that one,' she says. 'I just can't get through to her.' Goes on about Penny bunking off school all the time; about Jim, not being able to sort her out like he used to. 'She's got no respect for us any more. We can't control her – can't seem to control *anything*.' Says about Jim not being able to find work. 'But the worst thing is,' she says, 'nobody ever *listens* to what we've got to say.'

In a bit, I can hear her and Jim, rowing; hear the muffled shouting through the wall.

Then, Gran starts saying we didn't get any milk this morning and so she's getting on the phone to have a go at the dairy. And I tell her, we did – it's in the fridge – and she gets right shirty with me.

'Well, who put it in there?' she says. 'Because it wasn't *me*. Must've been *you*.' I don't bother arguing, even though I saw her do it.

She won't write me a note for games. Like, flatly refuses. To let me know who's boss.

'We all have to do things we don't want to,' she says. 'So you may as well get used to it.'

Huh. She knows how much I hate games. And anyway, if you ask me – whoever invented school changing rooms must've had a *big* problem. I mean, I don't actually want to take my clothes off in front of forty other people. And I certainly don't want to get in the shower with them.

I consider a bit of forgery, but can't even find a piece of notepaper and *she* won't give me any.

'I know what you're up to,' she says. 'A bit of a run around won't hurt – it'll be good for you.'

'Gran ... '

'Gran *nothin*',' she says. 'I'm not telling lies. You've got to do it and that's that.'

I think about skiving off. Sitting up on the bridge or having a wander in town. But then I think – sod it. Sod the bloody lot of 'em. I'll give 'em grief instead. Give as good as I get. Even the score

So. With the game of prattish rounders over, here I am, in all me glory.

And the water's trickling out, lukewarm like rain, and the best thing you can say about it, is that it's wet.

I shiver, hair dripping. Push it back, out of me eyes. Wipe me nose between finger and thumb, hoping nobody sees. Knowing I'll have a face like a deep-pan pizza, what with the concealer stuff washed off. But too proud to put more on in front of *that lot*; because I've got to make out it doesn't matter. That nothing matters.

I don't want *them* to see me naked. Make their comparisons. Discuss the merits of me pubic hair. Hip, waist, chest measurements. I've had enough of the tall, willowy, skin-and-bone girls – prancing around, chuffed as could be with what they've got to show. Giving me the once-over with their critical eyes. Whispering and giggling.

'Brunt the runt? She's too fat *not* to be a virgin!' Joanne Kelly remarks, her little clique snorting like it's the funniest thing ever uttered in the western world. Here we go again. Naked, wet and stupid. And any grief I was going to dish out is lost in a stutter.

'Grow up, will you?' I say, with all the force of a complete no-hoper.

'Well, *are* you? Or not?'

'Get lost.'

'Yes or no?'

I turn me back and they go into fits of laughing. 'Thought so!' Cackling away. And something inside of me is saying, *don't be weak, or they'll wear you down, wear you away.*

'Well, I'm *not*, actually,' I say, trying to sound superior, though not getting anywhere close to it. 'And haven't you heard – them that *talk* are them that don't *do*?'

But they just roar.

'What colour's the sky in your world?'

I dive out from under the water and for the towel. Wrap it round.

They follow on, behind. It's weird, they're mostly all

right to me, when they're each by themselves. Except for Kelly, that is. But in a group ... There's no let up.

'Tell us about it, then ... '

I feel ... I don't want to think about how I *feel*.

'Tell you *what*?' I say. 'Don't you *know* how it's done?'

'Huh. You're *clean*. For definite. And if you're not, it must've been a dark night or he wouldn't have managed it!' And they laugh their heads off again.

'She can dream ... ' someone adds.

They drop it. Start going on about last night. Who was around, who wasn't and why.

'Haven't you heard? Robbie got picked up and hauled down the station. Hadn't done anythin' – wasn't charged or nothin'. Said it was a right bit of fun winding 'em up, though.'

But they don't leave off for long. I'm dressed and on the way out.

'Got anythin' to smoke?'

'No.'

'Didn't think you would have ... ' Sarky as hell.

And that's *it*. That *does* it. It's like I can't see anything, I can't hear anything and I just *lose* it – turn around to Kelly and *smack her one*. Just like that. Whop – right in the chops and she falls back and one of her mates gets hold of me arms.

'Right!' she says. 'You've *had* it. You got it coming ...!' Everyone's crowding around to watch, then –

'*What's going on in here?*' It's Merryweather. Pushing her way in. 'What's the trouble?'

'Nothing ... Nothing ... ' They back off.

'Come on,' she says. 'Get moving. All of you.'

Everyone busies themselves.

'Me sister'll see you, later,' Kelly warns, and I'm gone.

I'm not one of those people who don't wish any harm on others. I wish they'd all drop down dead. Like *right now*. And I liked the look on Kelly's face as I was leaving, too. Dead ... stunned, she was. Yeah ... that's it, *stunned*.

Gran says she worries because I don't seem to have any friends. Says it's not right, not normal. That it's no good, being a loner. I tell her I *have* got friends – it's just she doesn't know them. Make up names to keep her happy. Keep her quiet and stop her worrying. I don't want her to know the truth.

Gran's doing the best she can for me; I know that. I need her. But it's still me *mum* I want.

Six

Mum's moving out tomorrow. To Paradise Found, or so she seems to think.

I catch her in the street, outside the flat. Just coming in from work. Watch her, walking across the grass. She looks knackered. Tatty. Looks like a cut-price mother.

I shout out to her.

'All right?' she says.

'Yeah. All right.'

Her heels are scraping against the path where she doesn't pick her feet up proper. Arms folded, she looks cross, even though she's not.

'What's on, then?' she asks.

'Nothing much.'

It feels funny. Odd.

It's the last time I'll walk up the sharp-edged stairs to our place. The last time she'll cuss about the pong and the litter. About the language scrawled on the wall. About the key, always jamming in the lock – and having to give the door a good kicking.

'We've been that stressed out, today,' she says. 'All of us – running around. Me bum hasn't touched a seat since breakfast.'

She works in a cafeteria; taking orders and making up meals. Egg and chips, sausage and chips, cod and chips, pie and chips.

'Chips, chips and bloody chips,' she says. She *reeks* of chips.

'Sit yourself down, if you can find anywhere ... '

The passageway and the kitchen are piled high with busting cardboard boxes. Bits and pieces poking out – clothes, shoes, the colander, the frying pan – blackened with grease, shoved in alongside her hair dryer and curling tongs.

'That's some of your stuff, over there,' she says, pointing. 'You may as well take it.'

Toys from years ago; a teddy with no eyes; half a plastic puzzle; a grotty Union Jack baseball cap with the peak bent backwards. The garish ornamental doll-cum-nightdress case she gave me one Christmas. Pleased as punch with it, she was.

'Throw it out,' I say.

'What d'you mean, throw it out?' Dead surprised, though I don't know why. 'Take it,' she says.

'No. Throw it out,' I say again and she tuts.

'You're just lazy, you,' coming to take a closer look. 'What about this?' Holding up a manky cream jewellery box, complete with ballerina, slowly rotating to the strains of *Swan Lake*. I don't answer and she puts it down again.

'What's it like, then?' I say. 'Dan's place?'

'Brilliant!' she says. Then guiltily revises it. 'Well, it's ... all right. Nice enough.'

'What sort of nice?'

'Well. You know the sort of thing ... I don't know really, how best to describe it.'

'A house ... '

'A house – modern – two bedrooms, kitchen, lounge. Nice bathroom. You know ... '

'Don't you think it's a bit soon?' I say. 'You've only known him a few months.'

'No,' she says. 'I don't think it's a bit soon. I don't want to wait. Can't see the point; I've spent half me life waiting. And anyway,' she says, 'you can spend *years* with somebody and then find out that you don't really *know* them at all.'

'What you gunna do though, if it doesn't work out?'

'It *will* work out.'

'But what if it doesn't?'

'If it doesn't ... I'll cross that bridge when I come to it. But it *will*.'

I shrug.

'You don't get on *that* well.'

'What d'you mean! We *do*,' she says. 'We get on all right.'

She takes the lid off the kettle, turns the tap on full blast. The water splashes in and out, up the tiles behind the sink. Except most of the tiles are missing; have fallen off with damp and with age.

'Anyway,' she says. 'I'm *sick* of it around here.'

'We could've tried for a transfer,' I say. 'Gone somewhere else.'

'No, we *couldn't*,' she says, firmly. 'If it was that easy, everybody'd be doing it, wouldn't they? We'd never've got past the starting line — wouldn't have stood a cat in hell's chance. And anyway — a transfer to *where*? To somewhere just like this ... ' She's fidgeting with her earrings. With her wrist watch. Then, eventually, 'You'll be happy,' she says, 'where you are; with your gran. It's right up her street.' Twisting her rings, picking at her nails so she doesn't have to look at *me*.

I hate her. I *hate* Dan.

I wish ...

'Would you tell me,' I say, 'if you knew where me dad was?'

'*What?*' She looks up, off guard.

'Would you tell me?'

'I *don't* know where he is.'

'But if you *did*?'

She thinks.

'No. I wouldn't,' she says, flat.

'Why? I want to find him,' I say. 'I want to *know* him.'

She forces a half-laugh. 'Well, he wouldn't want to know *you*, believe me.' Dismissive, like it's a big joke.

'You can't say that, not for sure.'

'I *can*,' she says. 'You'd only regret it. He's ... got nothing to *give*, that man. He only *takes*.' She stops. 'He only ... *grabs*. Was always *grabbing*.'

And for a second — even after all these years — I can see the bitterness seeping through. And I hope it leaves a nasty taste.

I tell her I can't stop long. Just thought I'd call in, see her before she goes.

'I'm not going *far*,' she says. 'I'm not going to the *moon* ... '

When we part, it's with few words that don't mean anything. See you soon, take care, and all that rubbish.

I walk home the long way. Avoiding the places I've seen Kelly's sister hanging out, on account I don't want my face smashed in.

Stand on the bridge. Looking back towards home. Wondering – when I'll see me mum again.

Feeling beaten up and angry inside.

The hazy sunshine can't blot out what this place is like; cheap, chaotic and destructive.

Part Two

Part Two

Seven

I don't know what this woman from Gran's work is on about to start with —

'No,' she says. 'She's not *ill*. She's *all right* — just a bit ... mixed up. Confused ... Didn't seem to know where she was ...' So they've shoved her in a minicab and sent her home. 'We thought we'd better phone and let you know. Explain ... '

When Gran gets back she's dead upset. Says they're talking nonsense; claptrap. Says they're just trying to get rid of her — but they needn't worry, 'cause she doesn't *want* the piddling job any more. She says they can 'stick it, stuff it, do what they like with it.'

But then she begins to cry. And I don't know what to do, or what to say to her.

She goes out into the kitchen.

'Leave me be,' she says. 'Just leave me be.'

Later on, we sit in the front room together. She's still in a funny mood, but not so bad. Harping on about the past, nineteen–fifty-something. How good things used to be; how much simpler life was then.

Tells me that the day Joey was born, it was that hot you could've fried an egg on the pavement.

'*Gran* ...' I say, laughing to meself.

'I'm telling you – it *was*,' she says. 'I remember it clear as could be.'

I just smile, let her carry on. Me gran's never let the truth stand in the way of a good story.

She starts going on about Grandad.

'He was a funny bugger. But we got on with it ...' Pauses. 'I don't miss him though. You don't when they're like he was: iron handed. *What he said – went,*' she sighs. 'Though any trouble between us was usually started by your mother. We had her too late; that was the problem ... '

'She said he used to slap her ... '

'He *never* did,' she says. 'Joey – but never *her*. She was always too crafty.' Stops again. 'He used to clout Joey all the time – was jealous, y'see, of a boy. I couldn't stop him ... I tried ... ' she tails off. Doesn't want to talk about him any more.

Goes back to her girlhood.

'We used to have some fun in them days. I was full of meself,' she says. 'Full of life.' But then her expression changes. 'Now look at me ... '

'We can get some help, Gran,' I say.

'Help?' she says. 'What for? *Olive Nelson has ample capacity to cope.* And don't *you* go saying otherwise.'

But she does need help. She needs *me*. As much as I need her.

She's a bit huffy. Tells me to phone the council – give them an ear-bashing about the broken pane in the window round the back.

'Ask them what they do all day,' she says. 'Because they don't *work*, that's for certain.'

Gran's an expert on work. A lifetime expert.

'Done it all,' she says, 'from scrubbing out lavatories to stitching overalls to wiping backsides.'

But she hasn't got a lot to show for it. Just a few tales, a few memories and laughs. And a life on the cheap. Cheap food, cheap clothes, cheap fags, cheap living.

If you talk about it, she always says, 'No – we never had a lot – *but my home's always been as clean as anybody's.*' As if that makes it somehow desirable.

Eight

Gran's mad that Mum never comes.

'She just can't be bothered.' Hurt that Joey doesn't come more often. 'He's a good boy,' she says. 'But he's so busy ... '

It's like she's sat here, waiting for a bit of life to come and find her.

When Joey does turn up, it's not before time. Though it is teatime, probably the wrong time, and definitely with the wrong girl on his arm, as far as Gran's concerned.

Peering out of the window.

'Who's *she*? Who's *that* he's got with him?'

The door is open with it being warm, and they waltz straight in. A waft of strong flowery perfume hangs in the air. Gran coughs.

'All right?' Joey says, beaming.

'Well, all things considered,' she says.

'This is Lorraine.' Dead chuffed with himself.

'Oh ...?' Giving her the once-over. Lorraine smiles, nods her head.

'Taking her to a job interview in town,' Joey says. 'Thought we'd call in.'

'Pleased to meet you,' Gran mutters, as if she's chewing a wasp.

'Hi,' Lorraine says, lifting her hand to give a little wave. Gran goes back to the spaghetti on toast, balanced on her lap. Turning it over with her fork; the dark orange sauce already spilled on the arm of the chair.

'Can't stop long,' he says, 'gotta be there at half-five.'

'Funny time for an interview ...What job's that, then?' Gran says, putting her plate down on the floor.

'Receptionist,' Lorraine squeaks. 'At Parkside Gym.'

'Oh!' Gran says, pooh poohing it. 'Not *real* work, then?' Lorraine looks embarrassed. Joey tuts.

'What've you been up to, anyway?' he asks.

'Me ...?' Not answering the question; eyeing Lorraine up and down. 'This and that. Don't you worry about me. I'm all right.' Lorraine flicks a sheet of dark hair from one side to the other, trying to smile pleasantly.

'So long as you are ...' Joey says.

'Have to be, don't I?' she says. Nodding at Lorraine, at the taut slice of flesh exposed between her crop top and jeans. 'But you'll catch your death, young lady ...'

'*Mother* ...' Joey says and Lorraine grins.

'It's the fashion ...' she says.

'Well, it wouldn't have done in my day,' Gran says. Then, half apologetic, half irritated, 'I can't offer you anything much to eat, I wasn't expecting company ...'

'We can't stop, anyhow,' Joey says. 'We're goin' in town,

then we're goin' out, later.'

'There might be a tin of soup if you want it ... '

'*No*,' he says. 'We don't want that, I told you.'

'Oh ... ' Gran says. 'Sorry I spoke ... '

'Just thought we'd pop in.' Looks at his watch. 'Best get moving, soon.'

Gran sighs. Starts laying it on thick.

'Pass me the paper love, will you? I can't get up, not again.' Sighs some more – like she's just run the London Marathon or something. 'I don't know what I'm gunna do with meself. Old age is a terrible thing ... ' But Joey doesn't bite. 'Still,' she adds, 'I'll just have to struggle on ... '

Lorraine asks if she can use the loo; check her face before they leave. As soon as she disappears, Gran asks Joey, 'Serious, is it?'

'Nah ...,' he says. 'You know me – just a laugh.'

She looks haughty.

'You be careful. You don't know where she's been.'

They're soon off and Gran's back at the window.

'I'll call in, in the week,' Joey shouts out from the car. 'Thursday or Friday.' But we both know she won't see anything of him for a few weeks now.

'Look at *her*,' she says. 'Thinks she's the cat's whiskers, that one. *Smelt* more like the dog's dinner. And did you see her stomach? Flat as a washboard, it was. No *shape*. Not *womanly*, at all.'

She writes on the calendar that Joey might come, Thursday or Friday. Hoping.

Mum hasn't been for ages. She sent a basket of fruit on Gran's birthday; phoned, to make sure it'd arrived; make sure she hadn't been ripped off. Gran said there were too many grapes. She doesn't like too many grapes – the pips get stuck in her teeth and she can't get them out.

Not like Joey. He bought her After Eights. A big pack. 'He remembers y'see – what I like.'

He's slipped her some cash and she sends me straight round to Mary's with it to pay off what she owes on the club book.

There's music thudding and kids screeching and screaming in the street.

Penny is sat on the step. Smoking a fag and staring into space.

'Lovely day, innit?' I say.

'Is it?' she says. 'Hadn't noticed ... ' Taps her ash onto the garden.

'Hot ... '

''Bout time. It is meant to be *summer*, after all.'

Mary's out, Penny says.

'Don't know when they'll be back. Don't care much, either.'

Tells me she's feeling rough. Went out with Jess and Mike last night. Again.

'Nutters, they are,' she says. 'You should've seen us – out of it, we were. *Right out of it.*'

She says it's a good crowd to hang around with.

'Nutters, though,' I say,

'Yeah,' she agrees. 'But *fun*. Though don't let on to me Mum – she thinks I went to the pictures.' Laughs. 'Probably thinks I went to see *Bambi* or something.'

Someone starts hollering, up the road.

'Turn that bloody noise down, d'you hear?'

It's Len from number twenty-five – shouting at Pam Mason's boys.

A couple of grinning faces appear from over the hedge; Carl and Andy. They flick V-signs – tell him to eff-off. Laugh.

'See you later, then,' I say to Penny, as Len starts on again.

'Silly old fool,' she says. 'See you.'

Gran's asleep in the chair. Snoring like she does, though reckons she doesn't.

I don't like leaving her on her own. But I'm bored brainless when I'm with her. And guilty when I'm not.

She wakes, all of a sudden. Gradually comes to. Starts talking.

'I don't know what I'd do without you,' she says, sitting there.

Says she doesn't know where the years have gone. Can't believe I'll be out to work next year.

She's heard there's jobs going at Farr's, the workwear factory. Says p'raps I'll be able to get something down there.

'Why don't you phone up – put your name on the list? Get a foot in the door ... ' She says you don't need exams – Maureen's daughter got in down there and she didn't have exams. 'They can't stop you – as soon as you're sixteen – they can't stop you leaving school.' Says they might train me on the machines – stitching, like she used to do. 'If you're good enough ... Plenty of overtime there, too. New boss is a bit of a bugger so I've been told – but cash is cash at the end of the day.'

But I don't want to work at Farr's. I'd rather have me eyes eaten out by maggots than work at Farr's.

She doesn't understand that, though.

'You're not in a position to turn your nose up at

anythin',' she says. 'And what d'you *think* you're goin' to be? The Prime Minister?'

'Course not,' I say. But I *do* want to be *somebody*.

'Somebody *else*,' she says. "That's what you want to be; and you're gunna have a rude awakening.' I try and explain, but she won't listen. 'You're as bad as your mother and too much like your father,' she says. 'He was a misty-eyed bugger. Head in the clouds ... '

And I just think it's weird. To think I might be like him. Yet don't even know him. Who he is. What he is.

And, y'know, they can't stop me from thinking ... Wouldn't it be good, if one day me dad turned up. Came for me.

Nine

You can take a short cut – through Briar's Lane Industrial Estate – to get to the Hill Road playing fields. Saves you going round by the precinct – but you still have to go along by the canal.

It's smelly in the heat. Stinks filthy; the water and the rubbish – though they reckon it's clean. Like, spotless, I'm sure.

I take a kick at the cider bottle that's in me way; but not at the baby's dirty nappy – decide to give that one a miss. Take-away cartons, chocolate and ice-cream wrappers are all blowing around in the breeze, under me feet.

A couple of lads are lying in the long grass, smoking, playing tinny sounding music on a ghetto blaster. Laughing, mucking around.

I came out early, to get away from Gran. She's up in the

air, flying at twenty-thousand feet.

'*Stop* going on about him,' she said.

'I only want to know about me *dad*.'

Said she doesn't know what's the matter with me, lately. That he's got 'nothing to do with anything.'

So. I'm in plenty time to be at the swings for eleven; to meet Mum.

These are *the* swings. Where she had her first kiss and I had me first ciggy. Nearly choked to death, I did. I thought you had to swallow the smoke, see; didn't realise you *breathe* it, inhale it. Had to keep practising in front of the mirror at home till I got the hang of it.

It's different here, now. Less rusty, more rustic. They've put up a fancy wooden fence – to keep the kids in and the dog shit out. Painted the benches dark green – school green – and stuck in a few bedding plants. Except they're ripped up and lying on the ground, shrivelled with the sun.

Someone's chalked on the wall, alongside the drinking fountain, 'Take a Break – Hang Yourself.'

Mum's early, too.

Decked out in sunglasses the size of saucers, she is. God knows what she thinks she looks like. P'raps she tried them on and couldn't get them off again – what with her hands being wedged in the pockets of her clingy, too-tight trousers. Strappy sandals are poking out at the bottom, completing the picture; how to mortify your offspring.

She's walking along, wiggly hipped and dopey. A complete embarrassment. Miles away in her thoughts. Looking like that, I wish she *was* miles away ...

Sees me.

'Oh – there you are,' she says. 'Thought you might've forgot.'

'Why would I forget?'

'Just thought you might. Might have something better t' do.'

I shrug.

'Where d'you want t' go then?' I say.

'Not fussed. Round the shops?'

'Haven't got any money.'

'Doesn't stop us looking ... '

'Haven't had any breakfast, yet,' I say. 'Let's get somethin' to eat.'

'All right then. We'll go down the cafe. Get a coffee.'

She walks next to me. Swinging a carrier bag at her side. Pushing her shades up on to her head, leaving a ridiculous red dent across the bridge of her nose.

She looks young compared to most other mothers with kids my age. Though not *better*. Spoiled by cloggy make-up and stupid clothes. She looks scratchy and rough – like someone you wouldn't push too far.

A couple of workmen stop digging their hole and gaze up; whistle, call out as we pass.

'Get yer kit off!'

I presume they're joking; or mad. She smiles and tuts. Says to me,

'And if I said, "Come on then, lads – where you taking me?" they'd run a mile. If not two.'

But she's chuffed, I can tell. It makes her walk with even more of a wiggle. Reddened nose in the air. Silly cow.

The cafe is quite busy. Full of old people with nothing else to do, and women with kids, getting out for a breather. Snarling — sometimes quietly and sometimes not — '*Ben* — leave your willy alone and don't spit in the sugar', '*Amy* — stop picking your scab and eat your bun,' that sort of thing. While the oldies look on, disapproving, not understanding.

'I'll pay,' Mum says, as if *I* was going to offer. Pulls out her blue leatherette purse, grabs a tray and joins the queue at the counter.

I bag the window seat. Hot as a greenhouse, it is, but nice. The sun streaming down, right on to me back. Showing up the sticky rings left on the tables by other people's mugs.

She comes over with drinks and a small packet of bourbon biscuits.

'So ... ' she says.

'So what?'

'I dunno. So ... anything. What've you been up to?'

'Nothing,' I say.

'You must've been doing *something*.'

'No, I haven't ... Nothing.'

She raises her eyebrows at me. Shifts in further on the padded bench seat.

'Your gran seemed well — on the phone.'

I shrug.

'You never come over ... '

'I know,' she says. 'I know. I've been so busy ...' Tails off, 'cause that's not the reason. 'I'm not exactly *popular* with her, am I? I mean, you could say — I don't get invited.'

'She'd like you to come. I know she would. She's said.'

'Well. We'll see. I just don't want it to backfire ... End up in another row. To be honest, whatever I do is *wrong*, as far as she's concerned.'

59

She takes a sip of her coffee, licking the foamy cream froth from her lips. Missing some, leaving herself with a thin moustache. But I don't let on. Ha!

'They're not very swift in here,' she says. 'Look at all the tables that need clearing. Wouldn't do in our place.'

Opens the biscuits, but doesn't take one.

'How's *Dan*?' I say.

'Don't say it like *that*.'

'Like *what*?'

'You know,' she says. 'The trouble with you and Dan is, you're too alike, you both want all the attention.'

'*What*? I'm *nothing* like Dan!'

She sighs, all superior and 'knowing'.

'In fact,' I say, 'I'd rather be *dead* than like Dan.'

'For heaven's sake,' she says. 'That's enough. Let's drop it, shall we?'

Well. Honestly. First, Gran says I'm like me dad. And now, I'm like *Dan*.

I don't want to be like anybody; I want to be *me*.

'What is it you want to tell me, anyway?' I say.

'Well, I'm not sure it's the right time, the mood you're in.'

'Come on,' I say. 'You can't say that, I'm here now.'

She picks up the carrier bag, plonks it on the table.

'What d'you think of these?'

I open the bag. Pull out a minute pair of baby blue jeans, a pack of three vests and the smallest socks.

'December the twenty-third is the date I've been given; so you should get a baby brother or sister in time for Christmas ... '

I look at her.

'What — *you*?'

'Yeah,' she laughs. '*Me!*' Carries on, 'So − you pleased then, or what? You always said you wanted a brother or a sister ... '

I feel gutted.

Don't know what to say. What does she *expect* me to say?

I hate her. *Hate her.*

'What d'*you* want a *baby* for?'

'Well, because I do. *We* do. It's ... a nice thing to do ... the next step.'

A lump comes up in me throat. She looks at me.

'Oh, come on,' she says. 'Don't spoil it. This is meant to be a happy time. Good news, for once.'

I tell her no, I don't want another coffee. No, I don't want anything to eat. No, I don't want to go window shopping. And no − I don't want her to buy me a 'little treat.'

I want ... I don't know what I want, any more.

And so she totters back to Dreamland in her high heels and a huff.

And I just walk around, searching. Searching for I don't know what.

Eventually, go and sit up on the bridge.

Think about what she told me once. About how it'd been − with her and me dad. How Gran had tried to warn her off him − but she didn't listen.

How she used to sneak out, meet him. Sometimes in town, in a gang. Sometimes, somewhere quiet, on their own.

How he seemed ... different. Made her feel good.

How he told her, 'Don't worry. It'll be all right.'

But it wasn't all right. And she ended up with me.

61

I'm just sat, with it all going round in me head. Trying not to think too hard. Trying not to care.

These kids that I sort of know, come over to me. Ask me for a light.

'You used to live on Elmside?' this girl says.

'Yeah.'

'Thought so. Thought I'd seen you.'

'Moved,' I say.

'Same here,' she says. 'Crap, innit?'

'Yeah,' I say. 'Crap.'

Ten

Mary offers to get Gran's shopping, but Gran's having none of it.

'What's the matter with people? D'they think I'm useless, or somethin'?'

'She was only trying to help,' I say. 'You could use some help ... '

'Go on, get out of it,' she says. 'Stop your fussing.'

Tells me to get on to the council again – about the window out the back. I remind her – they came, fixed it.

'You had a go at them for making such a mess, Gran ... '

'*When?*' she says. '*When* did I?'

She marches off outside to check.

Comes back. Upset. I pretend not to notice – don't want to make it worse.

'Get yourself ready for school,' she snaps. 'And no excuses.'

But I've already decided I'm not going. Not because of Gran, or anything. But because it's a waste of time. Because nothing at school seems to apply to me. It's just information that I can't do anything with. I'll go just *enough* – so Gran won't get into trouble, but I'm not going all the time, every day.

I tell her I'm stopping home because the teachers are striking. Not all of them – just some. Mine.

'First I've heard,' she says.

'They told us yesterday. And it was on the telly,' I say. 'But it's only a few of 'em.'

I tell her we'll have the morning together, if she wants.

'Well, I don't s'pose I've got much choice, have I?'

'No. I don't s'pose you have. Unless you chuck me out.'

'Can't be bothered,' she says. Flops down into the chair. Then eventually, 'I know what you can do for me. You can tidy them ornaments up. There – on the window ledge.'

I don't know what she thinks I'm going to do with them.

I put them in a line, blowing away any dust I can see. An Edwardian lady; a boy child with a tear rolling down his cheek; a kitten; a pair of robins on a branch.

'They're a bit ... naff, some of these, Gran,' I say, winding her up, like normal. 'Why don't you stuff 'em all in a box? Sling 'em on the tip?'

'*Naff?*' she says. '*Sling 'em on the tip?* You watch your tongue, my girl,' she winks. 'Or I'll rip your arms off, beat you with the soggy end.' That's her. That's the Gran I know.

I toss this chalky donkey into the air, catch it.

'Careful with that one!' she says. 'Got that on me honeymoon. Weymouth. Only holiday we ever had. Beautiful weather, she says. '*Beautiful* promenade ... Shame about the bridegroom.'

I put the little goldy statue of cupid on me head, see if I can walk without it falling off.

'Behave yourself,' she says. 'Bloody kids ... '

Take it off and put it down.

'D'you think Mum'll have a boy or a girl?' I say.

She shrugs.

'I just hope she knows what she's doing ... '

'I wonder if it'll be like me?' I say. 'What was I like — when I was a baby?'

'Oh, you know. Ten fingers, ten toes. Face like a slapped backside and a mouth like a foghorn,' she chuckles.

'Was I horrible?'

'Horrible?' She frowns. 'No baby's *horrible*. They're what you make them.'

I wonder then, why nobody — me dad or me mum — ever wanted me around?

Later on, Nat turns up with a new bloke, a smile on her face and a bag of doughnuts.

'This is Tony,' she says. 'He used to be a copper, but I've forgiven him.' Laughs.

'Pleased to meet you,' Gran says.

Tony looks dead embarrassed. Or maybe just *dead* ...

'Yeah ... ' he drones, in a voice that could well come from beyond the grave.

We sit there drinking tea, sticky fingered and sugary mouthed, Nat being unreal.

' ... and then, I said ... It's no good giving me an appointment next week, anythin' could've happened by then ... that's what I said, didn't I Tone?'

'Yeah,' he drones again.

''Cause, I mean, you've got t' be firm with these people, or you'll never get anywhere. It's right, innit Tone?'

'Yeah ... '

'I said to this woman – *I need some contraception, now*. And anyway, they got me in. There and then – so that just goes to show ... '

She comes up for air. Gran nodding in agreement as they both take a sip of tea, cups and saucers clinking. Tone's finished his in about two gulps.

'Want some more, Tone?' Nat asks him. 'Second thoughts, we can't stop, can we?' Not giving him a chance to answer. 'Going shopping; then we're off out tonight ...' she says to Gran. Takes another breath. 'How're *you* keeping, anyway, Olive?'

'I'm all right,' Gran says.

'Yeah? That's good; glad to hear it. And well, you've got Lise here, haven't you ... '

'She's a good girl,' Gran says. 'Most the time ... '

'Ahhh,' Nat goes, 'that's nice ...' Then, 'Anyway Tone – we better go. You think of me tonight mind, Olive – boogieing away on the dance floor – causing a storm and looking d–vine,' she squeals.

Nat and Tone go off down the path, arm in arm.

'God help us,' Gran says. '*God help us.*'

Eleven

I see these kids again; the ones I spoke to the other day. Sarah, Paul, Liam. They're down by the precinct.

Stand around a bit, to see if they say anything. Look in the video-shop window. Then at the noticeboard in the newsagent: 'Bike for Sale', 'Cot for Sale', 'Room Wanted'.

I wish I could get talking to them. Feel a bit of a prat. They probably think I am. So I walk on again. I don't care, anyway.

When I get home, Gran's really low.

She's got all her old photos out, spread over the sofa. They're loose and muddled. She's taking them, one by one, from a shoebox. Pictures of friends, pictures of family. Pictures of babies, pictures of Grandad. Of Joey and of Mum. Auntie Doreen. Auntie May. Small blurred images of Christmases, birthdays, anniversaries.

She used to look through them and laugh. But now

she's turning them over, serious, and sad.

'It was always in me mind,' she says, 'that somethin' would happen; our luck'd change. We'd come up on the Pools, or the horses ... Then it'd all be all right.' She sighs. 'Must've been stupid.'

I try and make light of it.

'What would you have done with it?' I say. 'Kept a pile of dosh under the bed and had sleepless nights ... '

'What would I have done with it?' She says. 'I'll tell you – it wouldn't've *changed* me – but it would've bought a bit of opportunity. That's what we lacked – *opportunity*.'

It makes me think. That me, Mum and Gran – we're not so different. We all want something better, if we're honest. Except it's too late for Gran.

Her grey hair is unbrushed, flat against her head. Clipped back with pins. She looks old. She looks ... the way you hope you never will.

Rummaging through the box. Looking for something.

'There he is,' she says. 'There he is.'

Hands me a small colour photo. A boy. Denim, head to toe. Bit of a looker in an old-fashioned sort of way. Bit of a lad.

'There's your father,' she says. 'Look after it. I haven't got another t' give you.'

I stare at the picture.

'Thanks,' I say. 'Thanks, Gran.'

Just sit there, staring at him.

Music suddenly starts blaring out from somewhere; you can't hear the words – only feel the beat; the bass line, vibrating.

'Thud, thud, thud,' she says. 'That's all we need,' throwing the lid on the box, hauling herself off the settee.

She flings the window wide open.

'Shut that noise up, Penny — or I'll tell your mother when she gets home.'

A couple of kids in the street laugh.

'What's up, Grandma?' they mock. Then start chanting, 'Turn it up, turn it up, turn it up ... '

She bangs the window shut.

'That's the trouble. No one's got any respect for anybody else.' Flops down again. Tired.

I go upstairs. Just staring at the photo. Trying to imagine ... Trying to bring him to life, see him move, hear him speak ...

Later, I tuck him safely away in the cover of a book — when it's time to make the tea for Gran.

'Something decent,' she wants. 'A nice pie ... '

But when I take it to her, she's asleep.

I try to wake her. She mumbles.

'Leave it there. I'll have it in a minute.'

I know she won't, but I put it on the table anyway. Mince and potatoes, getting cold. Stodgy and fatty.

I wonder where all the people in the photos are, these days? Now she needs them. Wonder, why they're not here?

I wonder where Mum is. What she's doing.

Sometimes, families are worth nothing. Less than nothing. Sometimes, they make the problems in the first place — the ones you're running away from.

Twelve

I don't want to look like a saddie, so when I see Sarah and that lot, I cut 'em dead. Like I'm *not interested*.

They're hanging around, down the shops.

I'm over the other side, going through me bag and pockets; looking for change to phone Gran. They reckon in the mini-market, that she owes for some meat. Put it on the slate, last month. She reckons she doesn't. Wants to know — what it was, when, and how much.

'*Liver and bacon?*' she says. 'They needn't think they can pull the wool over *my* eyes. I've *never* had liver and bacon from 'em. You tell 'em where to go.'

'But you signed for it, Gran. They showed me the book ... And we did have it ... '

'I *never* had it,' she says, nasty.

She's driving me mad. Doing things one minute, denying it the next. *She's driving me mad*. And I don't

70

know what to do. We need each other too much. And it scares me.

As I'm coming back across the road, Sarah calls out.

'All right?'

'All right.'

'What y' doin'?'

'Nothin'' I say. Take a sip from me drink. 'How about you?'

'Nothin' much,' she says. 'Give us a swig, will y'?' Holding out her hand for the can. I notice she has the name 'Paul' carved across her knuckles. She takes a mouthful. Offers it to Paul and then to Liam, who takes a gulp. Hands it back.

'Cheers.'

I feel uncomfortable; with meself. I bet I look stupid. Wish I looked ... different. Wish I *was* different. I bet they're thinking ...

'Got any smokes?' he says.

'Nah. But I'm just on me way to the shop ... '

He shrugs.

'S'all right. I'll get one off Dino in a minute ... '

Paul sits down on the wall. Pulls Sarah onto his lap. She squeals.

'Watch it ... '

I wish I had something to say. Something quick and clever and dry. But it doesn't happen.

'I gotta go,' Liam says.

'And me,' I say.

'See you around ... ' And he walks off. The others follow; laughing and larking around.

'See you ...' But they don't turn round.

Walking home, I go over it in me mind. What they

said. What I said. What I *should* have said. I bet I came across all ... wrong. Sounded dim. Pathetic.

I go straight upstairs.

Don't feel *so* bad. Until I look in the mirror. See the reflection staring back at me.

I look like a dopey kid. A daft, dopey kid.

Thirteen

Joanne Kelly and her lot are ripping into this girl called Serena. Giving her a load of grief; laughing.

I'm out of the picture since Serena came along. And people think I'm dead hard since I thumped Kelly. Even her sister didn't do anything ... But it's not just that.

Serena's deaf. She wears a hearing aid. They think it's the biggest joke in all the world. The funniest thing that's ever happened.

Shaping their mouths, overemphasising their words, shouting,

'I said — Serena — can you hear me?'

Serena can hear but doesn't answer. She wrings her hands. Drops her head and wrings her hands. But doesn't answer.

I wish I could do something. But the truth is, I'm not dead hard. I'm quaking in me shoes half the time.

We get a lesson on careers. On what we're going to 'do'. 'Be'. On what's 'available' to us, what's 'on offer'. But it seems to me that nothing's on offer. Nothing's worth having.

I skive off in the afternoon. Go and sit on the bridge for a bit. Then wander round.

Later, Gran wants me to stay in with her. She wants to teach me how to play cards. Crib and Gin Rummy.

'You'll enjoy it – once you know how. We can play for matchsticks, or pennies.'

Then she says Scrabble. What about a game of Scrabble?

'I'm not asking for much ... ' she says. 'I'm not asking you t' *fuss* over me. *Do* for me.'

But I don't want to stay in – I want to get out. I *have* to get out.

I say we'll do it when I get back.

'It'll be too late, then.'

'I won't be late,' I promise. 'I'm only going down the precinct for a bit.'

She scowls.

'You'll find yourself in trouble – hanging around down there.'

'Gran ...'

'I've seen 'em,' she says. 'I know what goes on. Wasn't born yesterday.'

'What?' I say. '*What goes on?*'

She doesn't answer because she doesn't know.

'Oh, go on,' she says. Dead narked. 'You're just like your mother.'

I slam the door. Cow.

But I can't help feeling guilty. Can't help feeling that

she shouldn't be on her own.

She's lonely. But *I'm* lonely, too. Not alone, but lonely.

I meet Brenda from round the corner – struggling back from the launderette, hugging an enormous green bag, stuffed full with washing.

'Handles have broken,' she says, rolling her eyes – her two little kids tagging behind, whining. 'Typical, innit?'

I smile.

'You're nearly home ... '

Someone's been round and sprayed black paint over all the street signs, so you can hardly read the names of the roads.

Someone else has set fire to a bin outside the off-licence. It's smouldering away, some bloke trying to douse it with a jug of water.

'*Idiots,*' he's muttering, to no one in particular. Gives me a dirty look as I go by – like, I'm young and I'm here, so I *must* be to blame for *something.*

Nobody's sat over on the wall tonight; they're all standing outside Video World. Arguing about a film they haven't seen. About how many million dollars it cost to make. Twenty? A hundred?

I stop and look at the display in the window. Read the posters.

As I turn round, Liam nods.

'All right?'

'All right.'

I stand there; holding up the wall.

It seems that Paul's got hold of some credit cards.

'Who the hell's "M. Davies"?' some kid says. And "T. Brown"?'

He shrugs.

'Spent anythin' yet?' somebody else asks.

'Not *yet*,' he says, as if he intends to.

Everyone wants to see – though they pretend not to be *that* impressed. But Paul knows they are, and is showing them off like a trophy.

Then someone says, 'Did you hear about Mason? Sold his mother's wedding ring ... '

'He didn't ...?' A mixture of disbelief and laughter.

'He did. Got fifteen quid down the market. She went to buy it back but the bloke wanted seventy-five. Said he bought it in good faith. She got the police and all, but the bloke was gone by then.'

'That's really *tight*,' Sarah says.

Somebody else starts boasting that they're in line for a job – a decent job.

'Fork-lift driving – I can make four or five hundred a week, *easy*. Me uncle's gunna get me in.'

And the others join in – going on about hearsay jobs with fat pay cheques – that they're *definitely* in the running for; *maybe*.

'Crap,' another says. 'It's all crap.'

They ignore him. But everything they talk about is *next year, after Christmas*. Never *now*. All p'raps, maybe and might.

Sarah says she's going to look after kids. For some rich family who'll take her on cruises to the Caribbean.

'I read about it,' she says. 'And I've sent off for the details – should hear back, soon.'

'You don't know nothin' about kids,' Paul says.

'Well, it's easy, innit?' she says. 'Looking after kids ... '

He shrugs, wiping his nose in the arm of his jacket.

'You gotta have exams for it,' some girl says.

'What – to look after kids?' another says. 'You *haven't*. That's stupid.'

They talk about going up the arcades on Friday night. Mostly 'might do's' and 'depends'.

Liam says he's going up.

'For a laugh ...' Pulling his hood up, and his sleeves down to cover his hands.

And I'm just standing there. On the outside; listening. Hoping I'll get a chance ...

It's spitting with rain. Getting dark, too. Then,

'Come on,' Sarah says to Paul. 'Let's go.'

It starts everyone else off –

'Yeah – I gotta go ... '

'Me, too ... '

'See you lot, tomorra ... '

And I don't want to look like some sad git that's got nowhere to go, nothing to do.

'See you,' I say, but it comes out dead quiet. Nobody seems to hear, anyway.

It's got colder and wet. I walk fast. Feel unsafe.

When I get home, Gran is still in the chair, dozing under her foul and fancy knitted blanket. She half opens her eyes.

'I was just gunna come looking for *you*.'

Oh yeah – sure she was ... Still, the thought gives me a shiver ... Of total and utter humiliation. I mean, *suicidal* humiliation.

She moves the cushion behind her neck. Settles down again.

'D'you want a game, then, Gran, or what?'

She's awake, but she doesn't answer.

I sit down by her. She does drop off, eventually.

I stay sitting. Watching her.

The corners of her mouth moistening with dribble. I get a tissue, wipe her chin; almost waking her, as her head flops forwards. She'd be better off in bed, but I daren't disturb her.

I wonder what she's been doing. She looks like she's been crying.

Fourteen

Gran says that 'lads are all the same', so I'm to watch meself.

I tell her – I'm not going looking for lads.

'No,' she says. 'But they'll be looking for the likes of *you*.'

She doesn't want me up the arcades. But knows she can't stop me.

Gives me two quid in loose change.

'And come straight home as soon as you've spent it,' she says. '*Don't* hang around.' Lurking there, as I'm getting ready.

Putting some make-up on – just a bit; a thin line under me eyes, and something on me lips. Then I brush me hair – this way, and that. Wishing I looked ... more like the others look. I wish I had their ways. Their clothes. Their confidence and their jokes.

'Now, remember what I said,' she warns, as I'm on the way out.

'Okay ... Okay ... Don't panic.'

There's always a right mixed bunch up the arcades. A few families, saddies and misfits. But mostly kids, on their own, or in groups.

No one I know. And I feel a prat, by meself.

The machines are ringing and singing and buzzing. There's a few winners and a lot of losers – shrieks of delight – cursing and cussing.

I try to look like I know what it's all about; drop a coin in the slot and press the button. Nothing happens, I press again. It rumbles a bit – and that's it – ripped right off.

Then I hear familiar voices – shouting and squawking.

'What's going on, then?'

Sarah, Paul, Liam, and a couple of others.

'Just lost ... ' I say.

'S'all right up here though, innit?' Sarah says.

'Yeah, all right,' I say.

'If you've got the dosh,' Paul says, stuffing his hands into empty pockets.

I look at Liam. He nods.

'All right?'

'All right.'

He's ... not like the others. Doesn't push himself forward. He's different.

Paul slips his arm around Sarah's waist and she responds by clamping her crimson lips to his. Eyes firmly shut, their heads writhing around. Liam throws them a look.

'I don't mind the *lust*,' he says, 'it's the *romance* I can't stand.'

80

I smile. They keep going, still intertwined – though Paul opens his eyes and sticks his fist out in a pretend punch, just connecting with Liam's jaw. Liam grins.

'When's the wedding, then? Can I be bridesmaid?'

Sarah's all right. We get talking, later on, outside.

She's exactly a year older than me. And I'll tell you what – she doesn't take any messing. Not from Paul, not from anybody.

She tells me that she lives with her mother and sisters, over near Highbury Road. That her dad's 'detained at Her Majesty's pleasure' – and her mum's not wasting time waiting for him.

'Good riddance,' she says. 'I think she's having it off with me uncle now, anyway. Me dad's brother. I caught them snogging ... '

This kid, Dean, pulls a bottle of white cider from inside his coat. Is passing it around.

'Here ... '

'Won't catch anythin', will I?' Liam says, taking a swig.

'Nothin' you haven't got already ... '

It's my turn.

'And no gobbing in the bottle,' he says. 'I know what women are like ... '

It tastes sharp and gassy. But not too bad; it gets better.

This couple walk past us; a proper Marks and Spencer pair. Walk around us, not wanting to get too close.

I hear them say something, about us being 'mono-syllabic'. And I just grin. Living up to what Tyson at school calls the 'colossal indifference of young people'. I mean, who *do* they think they are? Mr and Mrs *Jesus Christ*?

Paul is going on about his brother – how he rode his

motorbike right into their flat, engine roaring.

'*Right in*. Parked up in the front room ... ' And everyone snorts with laughter. 'The old dear – she *freaked* – nearly had a fit,' he says. At which point a little kid whizzes through us on a home-made go-cart.

'Watch it!' Sarah shouts, and this little 'un shouts back,

'Get out the way, then!' Like we shouldn't have been standing there.

We muck about. Have a laugh at everyone else's expense.

This kid called Worm announces that he's joining a band.

'What sort of band?' Liam asks.

'A *rock band*, stupid.'

'*Rock band?* Oh, yeah ... '

'What's wrong with *that*? I'm a born bass player, me,' he says.

'Since when?'

'It's in me blood, innit? Me old man used to play. Supported the Rubettes once, in the seventies.'

'The *Rubettes*?' Liam groans. 'Who the hell are the Rubettes?'

'What's this band of yours called, then?' Sarah wants to know.

'Well, we haven't got as far as a name yet – we're only just *forming*.'

She giggles.

'Worm the rock star ...?'

'You won't be laughing,' he says. 'You'll be sick – when we're doing *Top of the Pops* – and you're still stood here. We've got a brand new sound. The old man reckons we'll get a deal in no time.'

But everyone's laughing.

'Give us a demo then ... '

'Yeah – let's hear this *brand new sound* ... '

'Can't, can I?' he says. 'Haven't got me guitar.'

'Where is it then?'

'Home. In me bedroom.'

'Still in the shop, more like.'

'It's *home*. Not somethin' you carry around, is it?'

'Sing it, then,' Sarah says.

'Nah ... '

'Why not?'

'Don't feel like it.'

'Come on ... '

'Nah ... '

'There is no *new sound*,' Paul sniggers.

Worm stands up. Starts warbling, pretending to play an imaginary guitar.

' ... *she's so fine, just like wine, wish she was mine* ... '

We all fall about.

'Get out of here!' Liam says. 'Call that a song! A *new sound*?' he laughs.

'I never said I was a *vocalist*, did I?' Worm says 'You'll see – when we *make it* ... '

As he saunters off, he trips over his cowboy boots, up the pavement, and I think me and Sarah are going to wet ourselves laughing. Tears rolling down our faces.

Mr and Mrs J Christ walk by again – think we're laughing at them. Turn their perfect noses up, shake their sensible heads in disgust. Paul wolf whistles and calls out; they quicken their pace.

I wish they'd all stop going on about how skint they are; about how they've got 'things to do'. I don't want to

83

go home. Not yet. Want to stay here. For the night to go on.

I notice Joanne Kelly queuing for a burger across the street. She sees me and looks straight to the floor. I point her out to Sarah, tell her what a low-life she is.

'Oi,' she shouts over. 'Wanna start somethin'?' And we giggle as Kelly flicks her head and chews her lip, dead nervy.

But all too soon, I find meself walking home again.

They're good people to hang around with. Good people to know.

And tonight, just for a while, I felt like I was part of something. Like I belonged. Less invisible. More *alive*.

It's not late, but Gran ruins it all. Shrieks from the front step.

'What time d'you call *this*? Get in the house, *now*.'

Fifteen

In the morning, Gran's up and about early.

'Come on, move yourself,' she says. 'We've got things to do.'

'Later,' I say, from under the bedclothes.

'Now!' she says. Waits a bit. '*Now!*'

'Why? What's the hurry?'

'Got a surprise,' she says. 'Well. Not me, exactly. Nat ...'

'What about her?' Dead uninterested.

'She's tying the knot ...'

'What?'

'This morning. Had t' keep it under wraps – in case *the maniac* found out ... spoiled it for her.' (The maniac being Nat's ex).

'What?'

'Is that all you can say? Come on. Move yourself.'

'Are you *sure*, Gran? Have you got this *right*?' Thinking

she must've dreamed it up during the night.

'If you'd been up, you'd know,' she says. 'Nat's already been round here twice this morning – all of a tizzy.'

'What's it got t' do with *me*?'

'You're *invited*.'

'No, I'm not ... Am I?'

'Yes. You are.'

'Why didn't you tell me before? How come I'm the last to find out?'

'You aren't – nobody – or nobody much, was told. She asked me to keep it quiet and I have. It's all been done on a *need to know* basis.'

'I'm glad I'm considered t' be so *trustworthy* ... ' I say. Lift me head up off the pillow. Still unconvinced it's happening.

I push the bedcovers off with me feet. Have a bit of a stretch. Swing me legs round, sit, then stand up.

Mary's in her back garden, pegging out a line of washing. I open the window and lean out.

'Mary ... What's going on?'

'Have you heard?' she says. 'Nat's getting hitched?'

Oh, no. Oh, God. I mean, a wedding? That's all I need, a bloody wedding. And I mean, I *could've* had *plans*, couldn't I?

'Make sure you have a wash,' Gran calls out. 'And what you gunna put on?'

I've got no intention of having a wash and I haven't *got anything* to put on.

'How about your school uniform?' she says.

'Get lost, Gran! I can't go in *that*!'

'Why can't you? It's smart.'

'*Smart! Smart!*' I can't believe she just said that. 'Gran ...

Can't you tell her I'm poorly? Been up all night with the screaming ab–dabs ...?'

'I certainly cannot.'

'Why not?'

'Come on,' she says. 'You'll enjoy it.'

There is *nothing* I would hate to do more, than go to a wedding this morning.

'I feel a bit sick, Gran ... '

'Shut up,' she says. 'Shut yourself up.'

I find a pair of black trousers with the side seam split, and an orange has–been top. It doesn't fit me properly. Nothing *ever* fits me properly.

'She wouldn't know, Gran, if you said ... '

'*Get dressed*,' she says, standing, hands on hips in the doorway.

'What's that on your head?' I say.

'What does it look like?'

'A cowpat.'

'It's a very expensive hat, actually. *Quality*. Mrs Hard-castle passed it on to me, when I was cleaning for her. *She* wore it to her son's wedding – a big affair; marquee and all.'

'Still looks like a cowpat ... '

I *dread* being seen in public with her.

'You're a fine one to talk, anyway,' she says. 'Girls today don't know *how* to dress – you all look like bag ladies. Now – make your bed and get downstairs.'

Walks off.

'*Make your bed and get downstairs*,' I mock. Call out, 'What time've we got t' be there?'

'Twelve.'

'*Twelve?*'

'On the dot.'

'Then why have you got me up *now*? And why're you prancing around with that bloody thing on your head? It's only ten past nine.'

I just don't see *why* I've got to go. It's not like it's gunna make any difference – I mean, they'll get spliced whether I'm there or not. And anyway, they'll probably be split up by the end of next week. And I would've got out of bed and wasted a Saturday for nothing.

Mary's downstairs. Her and Gran, faffing around – writing in this big, padded card they've bought between them. Two pandas, in full wedding regalia, kissing .

'I wanted to put something funny,' Mary says. 'Give her a laugh. But I couldn't think of anything, so I just put "All the best".'

'Ummm ... I think I'll put that, too,' Gran says. 'It sort of says it all. That, or "Best wishes" ... '

Just then, the woman herself appears.

'Got anythin' I can borrow? You know – somethin' old, somethin' new, somethin' borrowed, somethin' blue ... For luck.'

I reckon she'll need more than *luck*.

Gran gives her a crisp, pressed hanky from the drawer to stuff in her garter; which is, by all accounts, blue.

'A pleasure, Nat,' she says. 'A pleasure.'

They've all gone peculiar, if you ask me. Everyone seems ... excited. So ... optimistic, like it's Christmas. As if Nat getting married is going to change life as we know it: forget world politics – this is Nat from number twenty-nine taking the plunge.

'Still,' Gran says, momentarily coming back down to earth. 'It's early days yet. Hasn't known him five minutes.

And if she weds as many times as her mother did, we'll all end up with marzipan poisoning.'

Nat's hoping that by 'settling down and being respectable' she'll get her son back; out of care. Hoping they'll give her a chance, give her a break.

Everyone's rushing, though there's nothing to rush for. Ready, early.

Jim and Mary have booked a cab to the registry office; to share with me and Gran.

'What's that on your head, Olive?' Jim asks. 'A bird's nest?'

'That's enough, Jim,' Mary says. 'You look very nice, Olive.'

'Well, I thought so ... ' Gran says, truly believing it.

Mary is wearing the crimplene dress she always wears out – when they go to bingo and that. A different hand-bag, though, which she tells us she got up the market for £3.99.

'Only plastic. But I don't like leather, anyway; always smells ... '

Jim says it was a 'waste of bloody money' but nobody cares what Jim says.

Gran gets the front seat because she's old. Like she's earned the privilege or something. I'm at the back in the middle – wouldn't you just know it. Jim and Mary either side, arguing most of the way.

'She's *twenty-two* ... '

'She never is. She's not had her twenty-*first*, yet ... '

The blushless bride turns up in a resprayed pink Cortina and a creamy Littlewoods frock. A thin band of nylon lace in her hair, worn headband style. Fag in one hand and silk carnations in the other.

'Beautiful,' they all tell her. 'Beautiful.'

'Hope the ex isn't hiding behind a tree somewhere ....' Jim comments.

'Shhh,' Mary warns. 'If I've got t' tell you once more today ... '

But Nat goes along with it.

'Reckon he is?' she says, flicking V-signs towards the bushes. 'Still, plenty of men here to protect me, eh?'

Both Jim and the groom look uncomfortable. Tony leads us inside.

We sit down. Nobody talking, a lot of shuffling; feet and bums. Us lot, and a couple of Tony's mates.

Gran is twisting her wedding ring, looking blank, rattling a boiled sweet against her teeth.

Mary is pulling at her skirt, trying to make it longer, long enough to cover her slip properly. And Jim clears his throat, messes with his tie, loosening it.

'Do your top button up,' Mary hisses, hush hush.

'I haven't got a top button,' like a naughty schoolboy.

Tony looks edgy – and Nat giggles nervously as a couple of her mates arrive: Colleen and Jackie. Feigns shaking hands as we're led through to what Tony calls the execution room.

'Lovely,' Gran keeps muttering. 'Smashing.' Then, 'Nice flowers,' she says, to no one in particular. 'And look at the curtains – very swish – I like peach and grey.'

'Shut up, Gran,' I say. 'They're waiting to start.'

It goes dead quiet. Serious stuff.

Ten minutes flat and it's all over and done with. Would've been even quicker if Tony hadn't stumbled and stuttered – had any amount of trouble saying 'impediment'. And if Natalie hadn't turned round to wave, every few seconds.

Afterwards, they all sigh a lot. Smiling. And Gran, for one, has moist eyes.

I daren't ask what's so damn good about it ...

They have to hurry up and take photos because somebody else is waiting to come in. Popular, this marriage lark.

'May as well go down the pub,' Jim says.

'The first sensible thing anyone's said all day ...' Tone remarks.

The White Horse know we're coming; though there's no reception as such. No food, or anything like that. A pay–for–it–yourself–if–you–want–it affair; a knees–up on the cheap.

It's straight into a liquid lunch for now; pints for the men, halves for the women. Except Gran, who's on the sherry.

The men stay at the bar, talking about football and women. The women sit down, talking about kids and men.

It's boring. Dead boring; sitting there, listening to them all.

They talk money – how they haven't got any. They talk sex – how they don't want any. They talk about being put upon. They talk bargains – cheap this, cheap that .. And all I can think is – I'm *sick* of living in Cheap Street.

They talk about the last good wedding, the last good 'do'. About who got legless and what happened. Drinking and giggling and getting louder.

'Never mind. A good laugh ... This is what it's all about ... ' someone says.

And I just sit there.

'Don't be moody, Lise,' Gran whispers in a minute. '*Join in.*'

But I don't want to *join in*. I don't want to be like them.

They tease, saying I'll 'be next down the aisle' – as if I should be flattered. They poke fun. They tap their feet, swaying, singing along with the jukebox. Telling jokes that aren't funny. The air thick with the smell of spilt beer and empty lives.

This is what it's all about? I don't think so. I hope not.

Gran says, she doesn't know what's wrong with me. As if she's ashamed, embarrassed of me.

But there's got to be more to life than this.

Sixteen

I'm looking at the photo of me dad. I look at it all the time.

Wondering – what would've happened that night if he hadn't told Mum it'd 'be all right'? If he hadn't been so lazy – said – No, hang on ... I wouldn't have been born, that's what. P'raps it would've been better that way – that's what I think sometimes. He didn't want me; she didn't want me ...

It's stupid, but I lock meself in the bathroom to look at his picture 'cause I don't want anyone to catch me. Don't want anyone to know I care.

I've been in there when Dan phones. Tells us Mum's lost the baby.

Joey's here.

'Lost it? That was careless ... ' He says to me Gran, being clever. 'Left it up the shops, did she?'

'Shut it, Joey,' Gran says. 'Just shut it.'

Dan says she's 'going loony'. That he can't handle it. Doesn't know what to do with her ... Gran tells him,

'I'll come ... Give me a few minutes – I'll be there ... '

And I feel jealous. Jealous that Mum cares about the baby and jealous that Gran cares about Mum.

But then Dan phones back. Says, 'Can Lisa come? She wants Lisa to come ... '

At first Gran says we'll both go. Then she says, 'No, p'raps it's best if you go on your own.'

And I say I will. Right now.

Joey says he'll give me a lift.

He talks. I don't. He jokes. I won't. He laughs. I can't; tied up in knots.

We drive through town, radio blaring. Joey bad-mouthing the DJ, the songs, people on the pavement, people on the road.

He seems to know where he's going, though hasn't been before. Joey seems to know everything.

'It's gotta be somewhere around here,' pulling into a leafless little road; stopping. 'What number is it?'

'Thirty-two.'

'Oh – you can speak, then?' Counts along. 'Twenty-six, twenty-eight, thirty – that's it then, I reckon,' he says, pointing. 'The one on the corner.'

I get out of the car.

'Can you find your way back home?' he asks.

'Course I can, stupid,' I tell him.

It's all right, round here. But not so great.

A little rabbit-hutch house in the middle of other little rabbit-hutch houses. Smaller and older than I'd thought. Shabbier – not like some gleaming mansion or anything.

I cross the road. It's quiet. But the stone-chipped path isn't golden and posh like I'd imagined it. Just grey. Ordinary.

They've got a porch filled with half-dead plants and two plaster gnomes. A crass doorbell that plays a tune.

I ring and Dan's waiting. Lets me in, on his way out.

'In there,' he says, nodding. 'She's in the living room.'

Mum is laid out on a squashy velour sofa. Pink and brown and modern.

'All right?' she says.

'All right.'

The room is tiny, but not crowded. Apart from the chairs, there's just the telly, and an umbrella plant in a pink plastic pot. Clean, bland, sterile.

'Sit yourself down,' she says. Then, 'Not on the *floor* – what you sittin' on the *floor* for?'

'S'all right,' I say.

She shakes her head.

I ask her how she is – daft question – I can see. She's been crying.

She shrugs.

'I'm all right.' And starts again. Holding her face in her hands.

I don't know what to say. Feel embarrassed. Wish she'd stop it. Then,

'I'm being punished,' she says. 'That's what it is – I'm being punished.'

I don't feel like I can go over to her; comfort her. I just feel awkward. But I say – I don't think she's being punished. I don't think that's true. And that Gran said lots of people lose babies – like every hour, every day, and it's nothing – unless it's *your* baby, then it's …

But she isn't really listening.

Starts talking about when I was small. How good it *could've* been — if things had been different. If Dad had been different. If we'd lived somewhere decent ... If *she'd* been different, older. She rambles on and I think she's trying to say ... Sorry ... And I feel sad for her. But from a distance.

I feel like I'm intruding. I feel out of place. I don't wish I hadn't come, but I don't want to stay, either.

I ask her if she'll be all right. Make an excuse about why I can't stop with her for long. Say that I'm meeting someone, that I've promised ... She says it's all right. That Dan'll be back soon, probably.

She asks me if I'll come again and I say I will. Though I don't know if I will, or not. If I want to, or not. She turns away.

'See you, then?' she says.

'See you,' I say, and I'm out.

Start walking home; haven't got enough money for the bus.

Thinking about Mum, and the things I want, but can't have. Dad and Gran, and the things I want, but can't have. Looking in shop windows t' take me mind off it all. Seeing things I want but can't have.

Walk — for ages. For ever.

When I get down to the bridge it's all cordoned off; blue and white plastic tape. 'Police', it says.

A few people are hanging around. Just standing, watching, waiting.

'You can't go up there,' someone says to me. 'They won't let you through.'

'Why not? What's going on?'

'Someone's been attacked. A girl ... a young girl. That's what I've heard, anyway.'

I shudder.

Stand there, with them for a minute.

'They should know better,' someone else says, 'than to be up there on their own. Asking for it ...'

I feel sick. And sickened.

They carry on –

'Have they got him?'

'Nah ... doesn't seem like it.'

'Who was she?'

'Just some young girl ... taking a short cut.'

I race home.

'Gran ... ' I call. 'Gran ... '

She's sat on the settee.

'What?'

'Someone's been attacked – up on the bridge – a girl.'

'Never!' she says. But it doesn't seem to sink in. She's sat there, in a world of her own. Doesn't ask about Mum, or nothing. Just says, 'It wouldn't have happened during the war; not when the Americans were looking after us.'

Starts making up stories; lies. Not real lies. Just filling in bits she can't remember. Like how she didn't have anything to eat all day yesterday ... Rubbish.

But she's happy. Because I've said I'll stay in with her; play cards. Because I'm going to be here. Caught up in the tangle of dependence, love and resentment.

Part Three

Seventeen

The long grass is damp with summer drizzle, but sticks in me skin, sharp.

I don't know what I'm supposed to do. Liam knows what to do.

Doesn't kiss me, but knows exactly what to do. Is just getting on with it. But gently.

I'm not doing anything much: laid, pretty motionless, with him on top of me.

I feel scared but grown up. Wanted. *Really* wanted. Liam understands me ...

He's heavy and hot and looks different than usual. It doesn't hurt, like he said it might. It doesn't feel like anything, just ... weird.

I don't want him looking at me, but he does, every so often. Opens his eyes. Then he sort of shivers. Collapses on top of me with a sigh.

And it's finished. We've done it. Had sex and it's over.

He's still for a while, and even heavier than before. I feel self-conscious. But relieved.

I wonder if I'm Liam's girlfriend now? If we're together?

It starts spotting with rain.

'Well?' he says.

'Well what?'

'You know ... '

I think I know.

'It was crap,' I say.

'Cow,' he says, and I laugh.

He gets up. Rearranging his clothes, tucking his shirt in. Just sort of stands there, looking around, embarrassed.

There's nothing else to say.

I stand up. Brush the bits of grass off.

Then we start walking; him in front, me behind. I keep a distance on purpose – don't want him to think I'm too bothered. Don't want him to think I care that much about him.

He doesn't look at me as he speaks.

'Want a ciggy?' Pulling the pack from his top pocket, lighting up.

'Give us one, then ... ' I say.

He gives me his; lights another, and we carry on walking.

'We should've used something,' I say.

He takes a deep drag. Shrugs.

'Don't worry,' he says. 'It'll be all right.'

grab a livewire!

real life, real issues, real books, real bite

Rebellion, rows, love and sex . . . pushy boyfriends, fussy parents,
infuriating brothers and pests of sisters . . . body image, trust, fear
and hope . . . homelessness, bereavement, friends and foes . . .
raves and parties, teachers and bullies . . . identity, culture clash,
tension and fun . . . abuse, alcoholism, cults and survival . . . fat
thighs, hairy legs, hassle and angst . . . music, black issues, media
and politics . . . animal rights, environment, veggies and travel . . .
taking risks, standing up, shouting loud and breaking out . . .

. . . grab a Livewire!

For a free copy of our latest catalogue,
send a stamped addressed envelope to:

The Sales Department
Livewire Books
The Women's Press Ltd
34 Great Sutton Street
London EC1V 0DX
Tel: 0171 251 3007
Fax: 0171 608 1938

grab a livewire!

save £££s!!! with this voucher

Buy any of the following books and get
£1 off each book you buy! Post-free!

On the Rocks by Sandra Chick

I Never Told Her I Loved Her by Sandra Chick

Push Me, Pull Me by Sandra Chick

Between You & Me: Real-life Diaries and Letters by Women Writers edited by Charlotte Cole

Name _____

Address _____

_____

_____

Postcode _____

I would like:

—— copies of **On the Rocks** at £3.99 less £1 = £2.99

—— copies of **I Never Told Her I Loved Her** at £3.99 less £1 = £2.99

—— copies of **Push Me, Pull Me** at £2.95 less £1 = £1.95

—— copies of **Between You and Me** at £4.99 less £1 = £3.99

—— Livewire catalogue

Total enclosed £ _____

Do not send cash through the post. Send postal orders (from the Post Office) in pounds sterling or cheques made out to The Women's Press.

Send this form and your cheque or postal order to The Women's Press, 34 Great Sutton Street, London EC1V 0DX. Allow up to 28 days for delivery. **Do remember to fill in your name and address!**

This offer applies only in the UK to the books listed above, subject to availability. This voucher cannot be exchanged for cash. Cash value 0.0001p